Quiet Echo

When Loud Voices Divide,
Quiet Ones Bring Together

Susan Agatha Davis, Steve Levi, Rosi Muller,
John N. Wamatu, D.S.Pais, Magdel Roets,
Evan Swensen, Lois Swensen, and Rebecca Wetzler

PUBLICATION
CONSULTANTS
We Believe In The Power Of Authors

8370 Eleusis Drive, Anchorage, Alaska 99502-4630
books@publicationconsultants.com—www.publicationconsultants.com

ISBN Number: : 978-1-59433-662-1
eBook ISBN Number: 978-1-59433-717-8

Library of Congress Number: 2025931537

Copyright © 2025 _____
—First Edition—

Manufactured in the United States of America

In a world where stories are often bound by solitary authorship, *Quiet Echo: When Loud Voices Divide, Quiet Ones Bring Together* breaks new ground. This book, as intriguing in its formation as in its content, is the collaborative masterpiece of a group of writers, each unaware of the others' identities or numbers. Each writer was tasked with weekly assignments and completed them within a solitary hour. Though born in isolation, these fragments were seamlessly interwoven by artificial intelligence, directed by human oversight, ensuring that the narrative remains a pure and authentic product of human creativity.

CONTENTS

Prologue

There is noise, and there is quiet strength motivated by doing the right thing, the way we were taught to do by our elders and our faith. Discrimination is not inherent in human nature. It is a learned behavior driven by misguided thinking and emotional feelings such as hatred or jealousy. Our resolve is constantly tested when making a right or wrong choice. We don't always learn the difference at a young age.

Noise has been used historically to disrupt and excite, but it's just a mechanism to interrupt your deductive reasoning process, i.e., the ability to distinguish right from wrong. Still, the quiet drive of level-headed reason always emerges in resolving our conflicts.

We are not made perfect, nor do we make perfect decisions. Yet we possess the power and freedom to choose a better world for ourselves and others with the simple linear thought process, the quiet way. The constructive way. The way we were taught.

CHAPTER 1
ECHOES IN THE DARK

A shiver and sense of foreboding ran down her spine as Maryam Khan stepped out of the Deli Kitchen. She tugged her coat tighter around her shoulders, and it wasn't just from the cold. Her eyes scanned the empty streets, still damp from the afternoon rain, gleaming under the glow of the streetlights. It was a town suspended between moments, like a breath held just before an exhale. Ready to explode ever since the buses had arrived with the Afghan refugees, her thoughts had been restless.

The images of the tired faces, the worn clothes, the bundles clutched tightly to chests—these were things she recognized. They reminded her of stories her parents had shared, of their arrival in this country a generation ago.

She turned to lock the door, her fingers lingering on the key as she glanced across the street. The high school was supposed to be a temporary home for these newcomers. And yet, it was already becoming a focal point of the town's unease. She could feel it in the tense murmurs that floated through the Deli Kitchen, in the sidelong glances cast her way whenever she walked down Main Street.

As she walked away, Maryam took out her phone, tempted to call someone—anyone—to talk about what she'd seen. But who would she call? And what would she say? The town wasn't ready to listen. Instead, she slipped her phone back into her purse and hurried down the street, her footsteps echoing in the stillness.

Teresa Nikas sat in her kitchen, nursing a cup of tea as she gazed out the window. Her thoughts were tangled, a mess of conflicting emotions that she couldn't quite untangle. As a teacher, she'd always believed in the power of education to bridge divides and foster understanding. Lately, it felt like the town was pulling further apart, with each side retreating into its own corner.

"All of us are descendants of immigrants and refugees," she murmured, almost to herself. "Some of us more recent than others."

She thought about the new arrivals, the Afghan families trying to make sense of their new world. They had nothing but each other and whatever they'd managed to bring with them on those long, grueling journeys. Teresa remembered the first time she'd seen them, their faces lined with exhaustion but bright with hope. It had stirred something in her, something she hadn't felt in a long time.

Just then, her phone buzzed. She glanced at the screen—Avery Sullivan. A small smile tugged at her lips as she answered. "Avery, what a surprise."

"I needed to hear a friendly voice," Avery said, her tone warm but weary. "The school board's at it again. They're pushing this agenda, claiming it's for the good of the students, but it's just making things worse."

Teresa sighed. "Change is never easy, especially when people are scared. They cling to what they know, even if it doesn't serve them anymore."

"Tell me about it," Avery replied, a hint of frustration in her voice. "They're not even trying to hide it anymore. It's like they think we won't notice."

Teresa's grip on her mug tightened. "Maybe they don't care if we notice. But we can't let them scare us into silence. We've got to stand up for these kids—for everyone."

Avery was quiet momentarily, then said, "You're right. We must keep pushing, even when it feels like we're the only ones caring."

"We're not alone, Avery. Remember that." Teresa's voice was steady, but inside, she wondered if that was true.

Caleb Mercer leaned against the brick wall outside the VFW; his arms crossed over his chest. He watched as people passed by, their eyes sliding over him without a hint of recognition. Once, he'd been a part of this town's very core. But now, he felt like an outsider, a ghost haunting the edges of a world that had moved on without him.

He looked up as Lars Olson approached, his hands shoved deep into the pockets of his worn jacket. "Lars," Caleb greeted, nodding in acknowledgment.

Lars nodded back, his expression unreadable. "Caleb. Been a while."

"Yeah," Caleb replied, his gaze drifting back to the street. "Guess it has."

They stood in silence, the weight of unspoken words hanging between them. Finally, Caleb spoke, his tone bitter. "You ever wonder if we'll ever get back to how things were?"

Lars let out a long breath, his eyes fixed on a distant point. "Sometimes. But I'm not sure the way things were was all that great to begin with."

Caleb glanced at him, surprised. "What do you mean?"

"I mean," Lars replied, his voice soft but firm, "maybe this town was never as perfect as we thought. Maybe we just didn't see the cracks until now."

Caleb was silent, turning the thought over in his mind. It wasn't a comforting idea, but there was a truth to it that he couldn't ignore.

At home, Dr. Aisha Khalid sat beside her son's bed, watching as he drifted asleep. His small face was peaceful, starkly contrasting with the turmoil that had become a constant in her life. She stroked his hair, her heart heavy with love and fear. She wanted to protect and shield him from the world's harshness. But she knew that wasn't possible.

As she stood and walked to the door, her thoughts drifted to her patients, to the countless faces she saw each day, each one bearing its scars.

The clinic was supposed to be a place of healing, but lately, it felt like a battlefield where people came to fight their invisible wars.

A knock at the door pulled her from her thoughts. She opened it to find Maryam standing there, her expression anxious.

"Aisha," Maryam began, stepping inside. "I needed to talk to someone. I saw something tonight, and it's been bothering me."

Aisha closed the door behind her, gesturing for her friend to sit. "What happened?"

Maryam took a deep breath, recounting the scene outside the high school, the buses, the refugees, and the soldiers. As she spoke, Aisha felt a chill run through her. She knew that fear, that feeling of being watched, of being other.

"What are we going to do?" Maryam asked, her voice barely above a whisper.

Aisha reached out, taking her friend's hand. "We're going to stand by them, Maryam. We're going to make sure they know they're not alone."

Maryam nodded, her eyes filled with a quiet determination. "Thank you, Aisha. I needed to hear that."

George Khan sat in the dim light of his small, rented room, staring at the loaf of bread on the table. It had been Lars who brought it to him, a quiet gesture of kindness that George didn't know how to repay. Lars had been one of the few people who didn't look at him suspiciously after his release from prison. But even Lars had his limits.

George knew he couldn't keep living like this—dependent on scraps of kindness from others, forever marked by his past. He'd tried to find work, any work, but no one wanted to hire him. The doors had closed the moment they heard his name, and the rumors started swirling.

Twenty years behind bars had left its mark on him, and though he had paid his debt to society, it seemed Cedar Valley wasn't willing to let him move on. He wanted to prove himself and show everyone that he wasn't the man they thought he was, but every time he tried, it felt like the walls were closing around him.

His thoughts turned to his family—his parents and siblings—who still kept their distance. Maryam had been the last to cut ties, and though it had been years since they'd spoken, George couldn't help but hold onto the warmth of their shared memories. He still felt the sting of her rejection, but now that he was back in Cedar Valley, he found himself hoping for a second chance to rebuild the bond they once had. Despite everything, he believed the love and connection they had shared as family could overcome the wounds of the past.

He hadn't seen Maryam since she stopped visiting him in prison, but he heard about her from others. She was doing well, running the family deli, living her life as though he didn't exist. It hurt, but he couldn't blame her. He had brought shame to their family; that shame was hard to shake in a small town like Cedar Valley.

George sighed, running a hand through his hair. He needed to get out of this room, out of this life. But he didn't know how.

A knock at the door startled him, and he rose slowly to open it. When he did, he found Caleb Mercer standing on the other side with a hesitant smile.

"Hey, George," Caleb greeted, shifting awkwardly. "Mind if I come in?"

George stepped aside, letting Caleb enter. They hadn't spoken much since George's release, but there had always been a quiet understanding between them. Both men knew what it was like to be on the outside, looking in.

"I heard you're still looking for work," Caleb said, sitting down at the small table.

George nodded, sitting across from him. "Yeah. Not much luck."

Caleb scratched his chin, his eyes thoughtful. "I've got a lead. It's not much, but it's something. My buddy's looking for someone to help with some odd jobs. Nothing steady, but it could get your foot in the door."

George felt a flicker of hope. *It wasn't much, but it was a start.* "Thanks, Caleb. I appreciate it."

Caleb waved it off. "Don't mention it. We've all got to look out for each other, right?"

George nodded, though he wasn't sure he believed it. Cedar Valley hadn't exactly been kind to him since his return. But Caleb was different. He had his demons and reasons for being cast out by the town, and they shared a bond.

"I'll get in touch with my buddy tomorrow," Caleb said, standing. "You hang in there, George. Things'll turn around."

George watched as Caleb left, the door closing softly behind him. George felt a glimmer of hope for the first time in a long while. Maybe things would turn around. Maybe.

Chloe Papadakis walked across the campus, her eyes scanning the bustling crowd. She felt out of place, like an imposter in a world she didn't understand. Her father's words echoed in her mind, urging her to do her civic duty, to make her voice heard. But as she looked around, she wondered if her voice would ever matter.

She spotted a voter registration table, a cheerful girl with lime-green hair waving her over. Chloe hesitated, then approached, filling out the form with a sense of unease. As she handed it back, the girl offered her a button with the liberal candidate's face on it.

"Remember to vote for our candidate!" the girl said brightly.

Chloe took the button, her fingers curling around it. She felt a sudden urge to throw it away, to reject everything it represented. But instead, she slipped it into her pocket, a silent rebellion against the expectations that weighed on her.

As she walked away, she caught sight of Lars, standing on the edge of the quad, his gaze thoughtful. She raised a hand in greeting, remembering going to his hardware store many times over the years with her father. He returned it with a nod, a silent acknowledgment of the shared uncertainty that bound them together.

Dan Larson stood at the back of the church, watching as the last few ward members filed out. Just then, a familiar face appeared—Joe Phillips, a member who'd always been vocal about his opinions. Joe approached, his face set in a tight, determined expression.

"Dan, I don't know how you can stay so calm," Joe began, his tone sharp. "These newcomers… they're changing everything. I just don't feel safe in my own town anymore."

Dan placed a hand on Joe's shoulder, a gentle but firm gesture. "Joe, I understand your concerns. But remember, Christ taught us to welcome the stranger. Our duty is to show compassion, not fear."

Joe looked away; his jaw clenched. "It's hard to remember that when you feel like you're losing your home."

Dan's gaze softened. "Home is where we choose to love, Joe. Cedar Valley is big enough for us if we see it that way."

The small room where Dan sat was quiet, except for the soft clock ticking on the wall. He'd been asked to meet with President Taylor, the stake president, but he hadn't expected this.

"Dan," President Taylor began, his voice calm and steady, "we've prayed about this, and we feel that the Lord has called you to be the new Bishop of the Cedar Valley Ward."

Dan's heart raced, a mix of emotions swirling within him. Bishop? He'd always been dedicated to his faith, but this was different. This was a mantle he wasn't sure he could bear, especially now, with the town so divided and tensions running high.

"President Taylor," he started, choosing his words carefully, "I'm honored. But I can't help wondering if I'm the right man for this. There's so much going on in Cedar Valley—so much fear and division. I'm just a simple man trying to keep my family and my neighbors together."

President Taylor gave him a reassuring smile. "Dan, that's exactly why the Lord has called you. Cedar Valley needs someone who can guide them through these difficult times with kindness and understanding. We need a spiritual guide, and you've been that for as long as I've known you."

Dan took a deep breath, the weight of the responsibility settling on his shoulders. He thought of the Afghan families who had just arrived, the worried conversations he'd heard at the grocery store, and Joe Phillips' fearful words just the other day. He thought of his children growing up in a town that felt more like a battlefield than a community.

"Do you believe I can do this?" he asked, almost to himself.

President Taylor placed a hand on his shoulder. "The Lord believes you can. And I believe you can, too. You won't be alone, Dan. We'll be with you every step of the way."

After a long pause, Dan nodded, a quiet resolve settling over him. "Then I'll do it," he said softly. "I'll serve as bishop. I'll do my best to help Cedar Valley find peace again."

Dan felt the weight of his role settle onto his shoulders. He knew this path wouldn't be easy, but he was determined to walk it, one step at a time.

Dan stepped into the hallway outside the stake president's office, his footsteps echoing off the sterile walls. The conversation had been straightforward, the calling clear, but the weight of it now pressed down on him like a leaden cloak.

Bishop. He had accepted the mantle, yet his mind swirled with doubt. Cedar Valley Ward had become a microcosm of the town's broader turmoil, and as bishop, it would be his role to lead this fractured community. It wasn't just the political and racial tensions concerning him; it was the division he saw creeping into the hearts of his ward members.

He couldn't shake the image of the Afghan refugees being ushered into the old high school. He'd watched it happen, his heart heavy with conflicting emotions. There was so much fear in the town, so much suspicion—and yet the words of the prophet echoed in his mind: "Be a spiritual guide."

Dan rubbed his temples, feeling the weight of responsibility sinking deeper. He knew his wife, Rebecca, would be supportive, but he also knew what it would mean for their family. More time away from home, sleepless nights, and heartache as the tensions in Cedar Valley only grew. Still, he couldn't say no. Not to the Lord.

Tension in Cedar Valley was rising, and everyone could feel it. The cracks that had once been small were widening, and the people who called the town home were finding it harder and harder to bridge the gaps.

Dan Larson would be sustained as bishop on Sunday, and with that would come the burden of leading a ward—and a town—that was fracturing more every day. George Khan clung to the tiny thread of hope that Caleb had offered him, while Chloe Papadakis wrestled with the weight of choosing sides in a town she didn't fully understand.

The quiet echo of Cedar Valley had grown louder, and it was only a matter of time before it broke.

A QUIET REFLECTION

Cedar Valley's fractures were quietly revealed in the stillness of a town caught between change and resistance. Maryam's unease, Teresa's tangled emotions, Caleb's bitterness, Aisha's quiet determination, and George's longing for redemption reflected the town's struggles—moments of darkness tempered by sparks of hope.

This was a place where divisions felt insurmountable, yet each character possessed the potential for healing within them. Maryam's memories reminded her that resilience could bridge generations. Teresa's belief in education as a tool for understanding offered a glimpse of common ground. Adrift and searching, Caleb showed that even the smallest gestures could reignite hope. Aisha's unwavering compassion promised a way forward, while George's yearning to reclaim his place hinted at the power of second chances.

The seeds of Cedar Valley's transformation lay in their individual stories. The road ahead was uncertain, but perhaps a new foundation could be built in the quiet moments of reflection and connection—one rooted not in perfection but in progress.

CHAPTER 2
THE QUIET FRACTURE

Chloe Papadakis stood in the college quad, her eyes darting from one group of students to another. The campus was alive with energy from being young and full of ambition. But Chloe felt out of place, like a puzzle piece that didn't quite fit. *Her father's voice echoed in her mind, reminding her to do her civic duty, to register to vote.* She had done it, but the entire process had left her feeling hollow.

The voter registration table had been set up near the entrance, and the girl behind it—bright and cheerful, with lime-green hair and a smile seeming too big for her face—had pushed a button into Chloe's hand. "Remember to vote for our candidate!" she had chirped.

Chloe had taken the button, but it remained in her pocket, untouched. She wasn't sure where she stood on any of it—politics, life, her own beliefs. Her Greek Orthodox upbringing had instilled certain values in her, but now, faced with the world's complexities, those values felt distant, almost unreachable.

She wandered through the crowd, her thoughts swirling. Her father's words echoed in her mind: *It's your civic duty, Chloe. You've got to vote.*

But every time she thought about it, a knot formed in her stomach. She didn't want to choose a side. She didn't want to be part of the division tearing Cedar Valley apart.

Her political science professor had assigned a class discussion on current events, and Chloe dreaded it. The last time they'd discussed local politics; the room had devolved into heated arguments. She had stayed silent then, unsure where she stood or what she could contribute.

Walking past City Park, she paused to watch a few kids chasing each other near the newly installed swings. Their laughter contrasted with the tension Chloe felt brewing among the adults in town. A part of her longed to join the conversations—at school, community events, anywhere—but another part worried about saying the wrong thing. What if she offended someone? What if she revealed how little she understood?

Chloe sighed and adjusted her bag. For now, it was easier to stay on the sidelines, observing and listening, hoping she'd figure out where her voice belonged one day.

Her thoughts were interrupted by the sound of footsteps, and she looked up to see Lars Olson approaching, his face set in a frown. He was a familiar figure around campus since his hardware store was nearby.

"Hey," Chloe greeted, unsure of what else to say.

Lars nodded in acknowledgment but didn't stop. As he passed, their eyes met briefly, and Chloe saw a flash of something in his gaze—something that mirrored the uncertainty she felt inside. It was fleeting, but it was enough to remind her that she wasn't the only one struggling to navigate the growing divide in Cedar Valley; adults felt it, too.

She watched as Lars disappeared down the path, the tension in her chest easing slightly. Maybe she wasn't alone after all.

Cedar Valley wasn't the town it used to be. The division and growing unrest weighed on her, all the more so now that she was beginning her adult journey.

Caleb Mercer stood outside his small apartment, looking down the road to the now-closed factory where he had spent most of his civilian life after twelve years in military service. The fog wrapped around the factory's empty windows, giving it an eerie, abandoned feel.

Caleb had always prided himself on his work, on being a man who provided for his family and took care of his responsibilities. But ever since the factory shut down, he had felt adrift. He shoved his hands deep into his jacket pockets, the cool morning air biting at his skin.

He wasn't alone in his frustration. Many of his former co-workers had lost their jobs, and now they spent their days looking for work or drowning their sorrows in cheap beer. But it wasn't just the job loss that weighed on Caleb—it was the feeling that something much larger was happening in Cedar Valley and pulling the town apart at the seams. He saw the buses, too. More mouths for the town to feed. He and his wife could not qualify for city or state aid yet; they had applied when he first lost his job. Now that they had spent all his severance pay, his wife was applying again. Some of their arguments were over his pride; he did not want to grovel for help again. She was practical about it, while he was angry and bitter and refused to sign the application. He ate VFW's free meals, leaving her with meager grocery money so she could buy food mostly for herself. Involuntarily, his resentment grew for the newcomers. He had served in the Middle East; he saw their poverty and the brutality of the Taliban. He knew the interpreters and their families needed to get out. He did not know if the interpreter who taught him Pashto and Farsi got out. His chest felt the heavy weight of fear that his friend did not make it.

Standing there, deep in his suffocating grief, he spotted Dan Larson walking toward him, his shoulders hunched against the cold. Caleb hadn't spoken much to Dan since the announcement that he'd been called as the new Bishop of the Cedar Valley Ward.

"Caleb," Dan greeted as he approached, his breath visible in the chilly air.

"Dan," Caleb replied, nodding. There was a long pause between them, the kind of silence that had become common in Cedar Valley lately. However, Caleb silently welcomed the interruption to his morose thoughts.

"I wanted to talk to you about something," Dan said, his voice quiet but firm. "The church is going through some changes, and I've been thinking a lot about the town."

Caleb raised an eyebrow. "Changes?"

Dan nodded, his expression serious. "There's been division—both in the ward and the community. You know that as well as anyone. And now, with the refugees...people are afraid. But fear isn't going to solve anything."

Caleb shifted uncomfortably. "I don't know what to tell you, Dan. People are scared because they've got a reason to be. The factory's closed, the economy's tanking, and now we have more mouths to feed. People feel like they're losing control."

Dan's face softened. "I know it's hard. I do. But we have to remember that these refugees—they're people too. They've been through worse than we can imagine, and they're looking for a chance, just like we are."

Caleb frowned, unsure how to respond. He wasn't one to turn his back on people in need, but the world felt like it was spinning out of control, and it seemed easier to blame the newcomers than face the deeper issues plaguing Cedar Valley. "Hey, I know better than many in this town that they are suffering. I was there. But my military and factory buddies are suffering hardship, too." Too much suffering.

Dan placed a hand on Caleb's shoulder. "We need people like you, Caleb—people willing to stand up and show that kindness isn't a weakness. If we don't come together, we will lose more than just our jobs. We'll lose what makes this town worth living in."

Caleb nodded slowly, though his mind was far from settled. "People willing to stand up?" He scoffed. "You think that's me?" The tension between what he knew was right, and what felt easier, staying angry and isolated, gnawed at him.

Dan dropped his hand with a gentle smile. "You forget how long we have known each other. You hide your true self beneath your gruff armor, but I know you are still in there."

Maryam Khan stood at the counter of the Deli Kitchen, her fingers absently tracing the edge of a paper napkin. Business had slowed down in recent weeks, and the empty tables in the dining area were a testament to the unease that had settled over Cedar Valley. People were staying home more, venturing out only when necessary, and when they did, they weren't stopping by the deli.

She couldn't blame them, not entirely. The town was changing, and the fear of the unknown drove people apart. The arrival of the Afghan refugees had set something off in Cedar Valley, and while Maryam understood their struggle—after all, her parents had once been strangers in a new land—the rest of the town seemed to view them as a threat.

A threat to what, exactly, Maryam wasn't sure. She had not heard that the refugees were taking jobs from locals or causing trouble, but that didn't matter. The fact that they were different was enough. And now, the hostility was seeping into every corner of Cedar Valley, poisoning the air.

The bell above the door jingled, and Maryam looked up to see Aisha Khalid walk in, her usual calm demeanor marred by a tension that Maryam immediately recognized.

"Aisha," Maryam greeted, offering a small smile as her friend approached the counter. "How's everything at the clinic?"

Aisha sighed, brushing a loose strand of hair behind her ear. "Busy. Tense." She glanced around the empty deli. "How about here?"

Maryam shrugged. "Quiet. Too quiet."

Aisha nodded, leaning against the counter. "Seems like the whole town is holding its breath."

Maryam motioned for Aisha to follow her to one of the back tables. They sat down, and for a moment, neither spoke. The silence between them was comfortable, an unspoken understanding that both women carried heavy burdens.

"I saw the buses myself," Aisha said softly, breaking the silence. "The refugees."

Maryam's jaw tightened. "Yeah. They've been here for a few weeks; remember the night I came by to talk to you about them."

Aisha's eyes narrowed slightly. "I remember. And the town? How do you think people are reacting?"

Maryam let out a bitter laugh. "You know how it is. People are scared of what they don't understand. The refugees might as well be ghosts—they are rarely seen outside the school grounds, but that doesn't stop the rumors."

Aisha nodded; her expression grim. "It's the same at the clinic. People talk about how the town's changing, how they don't feel safe anymore." She paused, her fingers tapping lightly on the table. "I've noticed the stares, too, especially whenever a refugee is brought in for treatment. Our town's residents have barely hidden hostility and fear on their faces. And the stares are not just for the refugees anymore."

Maryam looked down at her hands, her heart heavy. She knew precisely what Aisha was talking about. The stares, the whispers—they'd been growing louder in recent weeks, aimed not just at the newcomers but at anyone who looked different, who didn't quite fit the mold. It's not how Cedar Valley used to be.

"I had someone at the market ask me where I was from the other day, like they had never seen me before in this small town," Maryam said, her voice low. "As if they didn't know."

Aisha's expression softened. "I'm sorry, Maryam."

Maryam shook her head. "It's not your fault. It's just...this town. I thought we were past this. I thought we were better than this."

Aisha sighed. "So did I."

They sat in silence for a moment, the weight of their shared experiences hanging heavy between them. Both women had seen Cedar Valley's best and worst, but lately, it seemed like the worst was winning.

"Do you ever wonder if it's worth it?" Aisha asked quietly, her voice barely above a whisper. "Staying here, I mean. Fighting for this town."

Maryam looked at her friend, her heart aching. "I do. But then I remembered why I was here. This is my home, Aisha. My family built this place. And I'm not going to let fear drive me out."

Aisha nodded, her eyes filled with quiet determination. "You're right. This is our home. And we have just as much of a right to be here as anyone else."

Maryam smiled, grateful for Aisha's strength. "We'll get through this. We've seen worse."

Aisha returned the smile, though it didn't quite reach her eyes. "I hope you're right."

Aisha returned to the clinic; her mind still heavy with her conversation with Maryam. The clinic was busy, as always, but there was a new tension in the air, one that Aisha couldn't ignore. The largest group of refugees she had seen yet was waiting for care. The normal hum of polite conversation amongst strangers was missing. Instead, there was a silence heavy with mistrust and fear.

She had seen fear, suspicion, and even hostility in her patients' eyes. It wasn't directed at her, not outright, but it was there, lurking just beneath the surface. And it wasn't just the refugees who were the targets of that fear. It was anyone different.

Aisha had always prided herself on remaining calm in the face of adversity. She had been through more than most people could imagine—growing up as a Muslim post-9/11 when palpable hatred of Muslims took years to calm; she was raising her son as a single mother and navigating the complexities of being a professional woman of color in a predominantly white town—her competent and compassionate manner as a physician had quickly won over most of the community. But this unease felt different. This felt like something that could tear Cedar Valley apart if it wasn't addressed.

As she moved through her day, checking on patients and reviewing charts, she couldn't shake the feeling that things were coming to a head. The tension in the town was palpable, and Aisha knew it was only a matter of time before it boiled over.

It wasn't until later that evening, after the clinic had closed that Aisha allowed herself to think about what that would mean. What would happen when the fear and suspicion that had been brewing finally exploded? Would the town be able to recover, or would it tear itself apart, leaving behind only the fragments of what had once been a close-knit community?

She had no answers, but as she drove home, her mind returned to her conversation with Maryam. They weren't just fighting for themselves—they were fighting for the soul of Cedar Valley. And they weren't alone. There were others, like Dan Larson and Teresa Nikas, who were trying to hold the town together to bridge the widening gap between its people.

But was it enough? Aisha wasn't sure.

As she pulled into her driveway, she caught sight of her son playing in the front yard. He looked up as she got out of the car, his face lighting up with a smile that melted the tension in her chest, if only for a moment.

"Hey, Mom!" he called, running toward her.

Aisha smiled, pulling him into a hug. "Hey, kiddo. How was your day?"

"It was good," he said, his voice muffled against her shoulder. "We played soccer at recess, and I scored a goal!"

Aisha laughed, ruffling his hair. "That's my boy."

As they walked inside together, Aisha couldn't help but think about the future—his future. She had always believed that Cedar Valley was a good place to raise her son, a place where he could grow up surrounded by people who cared about him. But now, she wasn't so sure.

Things were changing, and Aisha didn't know what that would mean for her family. But one thing was certain: she wouldn't let fear drive her away. Cedar Valley was her home, and she would fight for it—for her son, Maryam, and everyone who called it home.

The quiet echo of Cedar Valley was growing louder, and Aisha knew it was only a matter of time before it reached a crescendo. But she wasn't going to let that stop her. She would stand her ground, no matter what came next.

Teresa Nikas sat at her desk, staring at the list of students' names. The morning sunlight filtered through the blinds, casting long, thin shadows over the papers. She had spent the better part of the weekend trying to make sense of the growing tension in her classroom.

It had started small—snide remarks, pointed comments. But now, it was escalating. Students who used to be friends were turning on each other, and Teresa could see the divide growing deeper with each passing day. It was happening in the town, and now it was happening in her classroom.

The door to her classroom opened, and Avery Sullivan stepped inside, her face flushed from the cold.

"Teresa," Avery said, closing the door behind her. "I've been thinking about what you said—about standing up for the students. We need to do something, and we need to do it now."

Teresa sighed, rubbing her temples. "I know, Avery. But it's not just about the students. It's the whole town. People are scared, and when they're scared, they lash out."

"That's exactly why we need to be proactive," Avery insisted. "We can't let this tension continue to fester. We need to address it head-on."

Teresa leaned back in her chair, thinking. "But how? How do we address something deeply ingrained in most people's minds, being afraid of the unknown? The fear, the anger—it won't go away just because we want it to."

Avery crossed her arms, her determination clear. "We start by talking about it. Openly. Honestly. We bring the students together; we encourage them to talk and share their fears and hopes. We can't fix everything, but we can start by creating a space where they feel heard."

Teresa offered, "We need a motto, Avery, and a forum for students to talk openly. They can address their fears and feelings about silent parents, hostile faces, things that have evolved since the Afghans arrived." They managed a mutual smile, a good start but with possible ramifications, which they were tired of using as an excuse to remain passive.

"How about something like this," Avery began, "Be honest and sincere, and you'll always conquer fear."

"That's good! You know, it's like handling hot peppers. When you remove the seeds, you remove the burn. Hate is like hot pepper seeds. You can store them in a dark place, but you must always be careful with them because they will germinate exposed to the right elements." This felt like such dicey ground. "Maybe we could start with a paper, an ungraded paper. Let's say a story going back two or three generations.

That early generation ought to hit gold. What language did they speak? Did they have a definite destination? Were they joining relatives?"

"Yes!" chimed Avery, "and what were their occupations or trades? That's all pretty neutral, isn't it?"

"Boy, I hope so. I'm still scared, but it sounds like something they might write for English class, or we could also call it a history assignment."

Teresa nodded slowly. Avery was right. They couldn't fix everything, but they could start somewhere. And maybe, just maybe, that would be enough to spark a change in Cedar Valley.

Dan Larson sat in his study, the soft glow of the desk lamp casting a warm light on the letters scattered across his desk. He had been poring over notes from church members, each one more urgent than the last. The divisions in Cedar Valley were growing deeper, and as the new bishop, Dan felt the weight of it all.

He leaned back in his chair, rubbing his temples as the stress of the day caught up with him. His thoughts turned to George, the man he had been trying to help since his release. Dan had always believed in forgiveness and second chances, but it seemed that not everyone in Cedar Valley shared that belief.

His phone buzzed, breaking the silence. He glanced at the screen— yet another conversation with the stake presidency, this time about the growing unrest in the community. Even the Church couldn't escape the tensions tearing Cedar Valley apart.

Dan sighed and set the phone down, leaning back in his chair again. How could he bring peace to a town that seemed determined to fracture further? The answer eluded him, but he knew he couldn't give up. The Lord had called him to lead, and he would do his best to fulfill that call, even if it meant facing challenges he wasn't sure he was prepared for.

☐ A QUIET REFLECTION

The fractures in Cedar Valley ran deep, etched into its streets, homes, and hearts. Yet, amidst the unease, small moments of courage and understanding hinted at the possibility of healing. Chloe's quiet search for belonging, Caleb's inner struggle between fear and hope, and Maryam's steadfast refusal to let fear dictate her life reflected the challenges faced by a town grappling with change.

Each character carried a piece of the puzzle that could rebuild Cedar Valley. Chloe's uncertainty mirrored the fears of many, yet her small steps toward connection showed the bravery required to face the unknown. Caleb's hesitance to embrace the refugees reminded him—and the town—that kindness is not a weakness but a strength. Maryam and Aisha's quiet resilience stood as a reminder that home is not simply where you live but what you create, even in the face of hostility.

These small acts of courage and connection were the first threads in weaving a stronger community. Though Cedar Valley's fractures were far from healed, these moments laid the groundwork for something more significant—a quiet but powerful movement toward unity, reminding everyone that even the most profound divisions can be bridged when individuals choose hope over fear.

CHAPTER 3
ECHOES IN THE SHADOWS

Teresa Nikas adjusted her glasses and took a deep breath before entering the crowded high school hallway. She had spent most of the night refining today's assignment, replaying her conversation with Avery over and over in her mind, dissecting each detail and potential reaction. The idea they'd come up with—to dig into family histories and trace common roots—felt both profoundly hopeful and frighteningly naive. Given the town's palpable unease, Teresa couldn't help but wonder if it was too much to ask of these students.

"Ready for this?" Avery's voice pulled her out of her thoughts, grounding her. She was standing close by, her arms folded but her face radiating the steady resolve that had kept Teresa grounded over the last few months.

"As ready as I'll ever be." Teresa forced a smile, but her eyes showed a glimmer of doubt. "Do you think they'll understand why we're doing this?"

Avery shrugged, though her tone remained optimistic. "Maybe not at first. But if even one student sees the world a bit differently after this, I'd say it's worth it. Remember, *Be honest and sincere, and you'll always conquer fear.*"

Teresa nodded, her resolve settling. She cleared her throat, addressing the class as they shuffled into their seats, more focused on each other than on her. She could feel the restless energy simmering under their chatter, a dissonance that felt far too old for a group of teenagers.

"Alright, everyone. Today, we're starting something a bit different," Teresa began, her voice carrying over the low hum of conversation. She held up a thick, worn family history book—a relic from her grandparents, filled with pictures and handwritten notes in Greek. "We're going to look into our roots, our family histories."

A collective groan rippled through the room, but Teresa pressed on, her voice steady. "I know it might sound tedious, but hear me out. This isn't just about names and dates. I want you to ask your families about their journeys to get here. Find out what languages they spoke, the food they ate, the things they believed. You might be surprised by how much we all have in common."

A hand shot up in the back—Jason, a tall boy with a perpetually skeptical expression. "What if our family's been here forever?"

Avery stepped in, her tone gentle but firm. "Even those families have stories to tell, Jason. We all came from somewhere, even if it was generations ago. And the things that brought our families here, the reasons they stayed—those are things that connect us, even when we don't see it."

Jason rolled his eyes, but a flicker of interest sparked in a few other faces around the room. Teresa caught one of her quieter students, Lila, glancing at a photo on her desk—a worn snapshot of her grandmother. Teresa smiled softly, feeling a sliver of hope.

As class continued, Teresa and Avery guided them through discussions on migration, resilience, and survival. Also, the importance of indigenous people, explorers, colonization, and the reasons immigrants came to America were discussed. They encouraged them to think about the parallels between their ancestors and the Afghan refugees. And though they couldn't tell if the seeds they were planting would take root, they held onto the belief that understanding—even a tiny glimmer of it—might bring Cedar Valley closer together.

As they watched the students filter out of the classroom, Teresa turned to Avery, her voice low, "Do you think we're getting through to them? I worry we might be running out of time to really reach them." Avery nodded, sharing the weight of Teresa's concern.

Caleb spent the morning sipping coffee on a park bench. He had been "pushed" out of his apartment, leaving his breakfast to get cold on the kitchen table. It was all Helen, his wife's fault, of course—her constant nagging, although she didn't see it that way.

"You should get a psych exam," Helen had told him. "I'm serious. Then you can get some help. You might even get on disability. God knows we need the money." She was doing dishes and didn't look up until she heard the kitchen door slam. Sighing, she picked up his plate, wrapped the food, and put it in the fridge.

By now, she would be at work, and it would be safe to go back, Caleb thought. Coffee in hand, he stood up, stretched his legs, and began to walk home. He trudged through the thin sprinkling of snow, his body wrapped in a lightweight parka, and his eyes focused on the ground. He didn't hear the sedan pull up behind him until Dan Larson rolled down his window and yelled.

"It's cold out here. Need a ride?"

Startled, Caleb nearly tripped on the broken sidewalk. He turned to talk to Dan. "Nah. I'm fine. Just getting some fresh air." He straightened his back to try and look normal.

"Come on. Get in. I won't try to convert you. I promise." Dan had a warm smile and easy way about him that made Caleb feel safe, and Caleb never felt safe.

"It's not that far," Caleb continued to argue, eyeing the car and wondering how warm it was.

"I'm not going to ask again," Dan replied.

Pride surrendered to the idea of warmth, and Caleb got into the car. He set his coffee in the cup holder, fastened his seatbelt, and felt the heat surround him. "Nice ride."

"I bought it second-hand for my oldest daughter, but it needs an inspection and new tires, so I dropped her off at school. She tried to take my car instead, but I won't let that happen." Dan chuckled. "Kids."

Caleb frowned. He and Dan had gone to high school together, but that's where the similarity ended. "Kids," he agreed, even though he didn't have any.

The two men were quiet for a couple of minutes. Dan finally said, "I heard you speak their language." He didn't have to say who "they" were.

Caleb shrugged. "Somewhat. I'm not fluent though. Why?"

"Avery Sullivan called me. She wants to take some of her kids to the old school to see what the refugees are like. She wants to humanize them so the kids won't be scared. If the kids aren't scared, then their parents might relax, too." Dan spoke as if he supported the idea.

Caleb didn't. "You mean like in a zoo?" he asked in disdain.

It was Dan's turn to frown. "A zoo? What are you talking about?"

Rolling his eyes in irritation, Caleb explained. "She wants to take the kids to see the refugees—not the people, the refugees. She wants to "humanize" them as if they ain't humans already. She wants the kids to see how they live and what they do, like watching animals in a zoo. Bad idea. Insulting."

Dan pursed his lips before speaking again. "Do you have a better idea?"

"You should get that doctor woman to go over there and break the ice. You know, like talk to the refugees' head guy and see if they can work something out. Maybe a couple of 'em could go to the school and talk to the kids." Caleb glanced out the window and took a sip of his coffee. It was already cold.

"I tried. She doesn't want to go," Dan said. "At least not now. Besides, she's not Afghani she's Pakistani. She wants to help, but I think she may be a little afraid of them."

"Or afraid of how everyone else will treat her if she goes over there," said Caleb. "She probably speaks their language too. Pakistanis speak Farsi. If her parents wanted to preserve their heritage, they probably taught her though they live here."

Dan knew that Caleb was right. "You could go with her," Dan suggested.

"This is it." Caleb pointed to his apartment building. "Thanks for the lift." As soon as the car stopped, Caleb got out without saying another word, leaving his coffee cup behind.

Lars Olson stood at the entrance of his modest hardware store, gazing at the street with a weary detachment. The store, usually his pride and joy, felt like an anchor around his neck today. He sipped his bitter coffee, grimacing as the cold liquid settled on his tongue. Lately, everything seemed like it had lost its warmth, its spark. Cedar Valley, once a place where he could nod at a stranger and get a friendly wave in return, was becoming unrecognizable. It was as if a dense fog had settled over the town, clouding people's vision of each other.

He noticed the Voter Registration table on the corner across the street, a cheerful sign inviting people to make their voices heard. The sight only added to his unease. Voting used to feel like a civic duty, something meaningful. Now, it felt like a game rigged by those who held power, a hollow gesture that did little to address the real concerns weighing on him and others like him. The corner was between the college and the old high school. He cynically wondered how many refugees they had illegally registered to vote so far. He walked past the table when on errands, so he often overheard the cheerful girl with lime-green hair giving out buttons for the liberal candidate, telling the newly registered to vote for that person. Did she not know campaigning at voter registration was against the rules? His cynical self said she probably did know and did it anyway, not expecting anyone to confront them, given the country's hostile political environment toward certain disagreements.

Lars was no stranger to hard work—he'd built his life around it, pouring his energy into the store after inheriting it from his father. But the changes sweeping through the country, and now his town, made him feel like an outsider in the place he'd once felt rooted.

Lars had grown up believing America was the last, best hope for humanity, a land where democracy didn't just mean elections but a genuine opportunity for everyone. Watching his father, a first-generation immigrant from Norway, build their family's livelihood from the ground up instilled a sense of pride in him. But over the years, as he'd watched corporate giants swallow small businesses and seen politicians speak in platitudes without addressing the struggles of everyday people, that pride had faded into disillusionment.

Lost in thought, he was startled by a familiar voice. "Morning, Lars." Chloe Papadakis greeted him with a polite smile as she passed by on her way to school. He had seen her register to vote the other day.

"Off to change the world?" he asked, his tone a mixture of admiration and skepticism.

"Trying," she replied, offering him an encouraging smile before moving on.

Lars watched her go, a pang of longing flickering in his chest. It had been years since he'd felt that kind of purpose. Honestly, he was envious of anyone who still believed change was possible. He wanted to believe it, too, but life had taught him otherwise.

He let his gaze drift back to the street, catching sight of Maryam Khan weaving through the protest crowd outside the old high school. Now that it was common knowledge how many and where the refugees were, the town's people were making their frustrations heard at the source. Maryam was pulling her almost overflowing grocery wagon, containing sandwiches and fruit, her posture tense but determined. The sight stirred something in him—a memory of his mother, who had always insisted on helping others, even if they were strangers. She used to say that kindness was the glue holding communities together. It was a sentiment Lars had carried with him, though he sometimes felt like he was grasping at the frayed edges of that belief.

A couple of men nearby were muttering, their voices just loud enough for Lars to catch snippets. "Why don't they just go back?" one of them said. "This isn't their home."

"Not yet, anyway," replied the other with a sneer.

Lars clenched his jaw, his hand tightening around his coffee cup. He'd heard similar sentiments whispered around town lately, and every time, it felt like a crack spreading through the foundation of everything he valued.

Cedar Valley was supposed to be different. It was supposed to be a place where people looked out for each other, where neighbors meant something. But now, all he saw was a growing divide, and it tore at him.

He considered going over to the men for a moment, telling them off like his father might have done in his day. But he stopped himself. He knew it wouldn't change anything. The bitterness in people's hearts had grown roots, and he doubted a few harsh words from him would make a dent. So, he stood there, feeling the weight of his inaction settle over him like a shroud.

Just as he was about to turn back inside, he saw Dan Larson approaching, his face etched with worry. Lars nodded in greeting as Dan stopped beside him, both men watching the crowd in silence for a moment.

"Looks like things are getting worse," Dan muttered, almost to himself.

Lars nodded, his gaze never leaving the protesters. "Yeah. Seems like everyone's looking for someone to blame these days."

Dan glanced at him, a hint of curiosity in his eyes. "You ever think about getting involved, maybe trying to help bring people together?"

Lars let out a low chuckle, devoid of humor. "I used to think that was possible. These days, I'm not so sure." He took a long sip of his coffee, savoring its bitterness. "Sometimes, it feels like this town's already made up its mind. People are angry and scared, which leaves little room for anything else."

Dan nodded thoughtfully; his expression somber. "Maybe. But that doesn't mean we stop trying."

Lars met his gaze, a faint glimmer of something—hope, perhaps—stirring in his chest. "You're a good man, Dan. Better than most around here. But don't lose yourself trying to fix everyone else. Some things… some people…they don't want to be saved."

Dan's face softened. "Maybe they just don't know how."

Lars shrugged, unwilling to argue but unconvinced. He watched Dan head toward the high school, his shoulders squared, a man on a mission. Lars stayed where he was, rooted to the spot, feeling an ache in his chest that had nothing to do with age or fatigue. He wanted to believe Dan was right, and there was still something left to salvage in Cedar Valley.

As the crowd outside the old school grew louder, their voices echoing through the street, Lars retreated into his store. The world outside felt like it was unravelling, and he wasn't sure he had the strength to stitch it back together.

Lars looked around his hardware store, remembering when folks came in just to talk about the weather or ask his advice on fixing a broken fence. Now, conversations were hushed, tinged with tension. "Funny how things change," he thought, feeling his store had become a mirror of the town's unrest.

Maryam Khan faced a more physical than metaphorical storm outside the old high school. A crowd had gathered at the entrance, their placards and hastily scribbled signs a jumbled mix of messages—*Welcome Refugees* mingled with *Go Back to Where You Came From!*" The voices were just as divided, some supportive, others simmering with resentment and anger.

Gripping her coat tighter, Maryam carefully pulled the grocery wagon through the crowd as her heart raced. She had spent the morning preparing food for the Afghan refugees inside the school, hoping homemade sandwiches and fresh fruit would bring them comfort amid the turmoil. But as she approached the entrance, someone shouted from the crowd.

"Hey! She's one of them!"

Maryam felt her throat tighten, but she pressed forward, forcing herself to ignore the jeers. Her resolve wavered only for a moment when she felt something wet hit her back. She stopped, stunned, as the smell of coffee rose from her coat. Glancing over her shoulder, she saw a crumpled paper cup at her feet, brown liquid seeping into the ground.

"Go home!" a man yelled, his voice full of disdain.

Before Maryam could respond, a young man stepped forward, his face twisted with anger. "Leave her alone! She owns the Deli on Main Street, what's wrong with you?" he shouted at the man who'd thrown the coffee.

"Why should I?" the man sneered back. "She's just like them—thinks she's better than us."

The young man's fists clenched, and Maryam's heart sank as she saw his arm pull back. "Stop!" she cried, but it was too late. His fist connected with the man's jaw, and all at once, chaos erupted.

People surged forward, some shouting in support of Maryam, others yelling insults. Fists flew, and the crowd turned into a writhing mass of anger and frustration. Someone shoved Maryam to the side, and she stumbled, losing her grip on the handle of the wagon and, to her horror, it toppled over. The carefully prepared food scattered across the ground, trampled underfoot as the crowd surged around her.

Just as she was about to retreat, sirens cut through the noise. Police cars pulled up, and officers poured out, shouting for the crowd to disperse. One officer grabbed Maryam by the arm, pulling her to safety as the police pushed into the crowd, trying to separate the fighting men and women.

"Are you alright, ma'am?" the officer asked, his voice tense but concerned.

Maryam nodded, her voice barely a whisper. "Yes, thank you."

The officer nodded, then returned to the crowd, calling for calm. Breathless, Dan arrived by Maryam's side.

"Are you okay?!"

Maryam slowed her breathing and answered stressfully. "Physically, okay. Emotionally, I'm heartbroken."

Dan agreed. "This has gone too far. We have to figure out a path to community unity."

Together, they watched as the police managed to pull the brawling individuals apart, the crowd slowly dispersing under the officers' stern gazes. The scene left Maryam shaken, her heart heavy with the weight of what had just unfolded.

As she stood there, staring at the scattered sandwiches, the realization hit her like a punch to the gut: hatred and resentment had taken root in Cedar Valley, spreading. And if it wasn't stopped, she feared it would consume them all.

Feeling defeated, Maryam asked, "Dan, will you help me clean this mess up?"

"Of course."

They began picking up the trampled food, symbolic of how they knew the trampled community needed to be picked up from its division.

George's day had started with a flicker of hope, a feeling he hadn't experienced in years. He'd been promised a job interview, a chance to rebuild. But by the time he returned home, his spirits were in tatters, weighed down by the rejection and ridicule he'd faced. Jailbird. They'd called him that to his face, sneering as they turned him away.

Humming a hymn under his breath, he tried to cling to the remnants of his faith, but it felt like sand slipping through his fingers. Desperate for something—anything—to hold onto, he flung himself onto his bed, covering his head with a worn blanket, hoping to shut out the world.

The shrill ring of his phone shattered the silence. He answered, voice hollow. "Hello?"

"Hi, George, it's Dan. I hope I'm not catching you at a bad time. I'd like to schedule a meeting for us at my office soon. There's something I'd like to discuss with you."

George hesitated, taken aback. "Uh...sure, Dan. I'll be there."

Hanging up after agreeing on a date and time, George felt a spark reignite in his heart. He did not know what Dan wanted, but just having him reach out gave him hope. It wasn't much, but maybe it was enough to keep him going a little longer.

Maryam retreated to the small, private space at the back of her deli, seeking solace in the familiar prayer ritual. The turmoil outside weighed heavily on her, watching the good people of her town allow fear to turn friendly neighbors into angry strangers. Her thoughts tangled with concern for the refugees whose struggles mirrored her own family's journey and with her private, tightly held worry for how her brother was navigating this tension in the community. She knew that though George had paid dearly for poor decisions in his youth by being incarcerated for twenty years and continued to be shunned by his family, Cedar Valley residents felt the same about him as they did about the refugees. The town wanted them gone. For her, why was it easier to reach out to strangers than to her own brother?

"Oh, dear Lord," she whispered, her voice thick with emotion. "Please guide me. Help me."

Aisha Khalid tightened her grip on the steering wheel as she drove toward the clinic, her mind swirling with the usual worries but punctuated by a growing sense of urgency. Every day, it seemed the subtle tension in Cedar Valley edged closer to breaking. The morning mist clung to the hillsides, reflecting the town's subdued and wary mood. She passed familiar sights—the diner, the park where children once played freely—but now even these places seemed tainted, their innocence overshadowed by distrustful glances and whispered conversations.

As Aisha pulled into the parking lot, she noticed a familiar figure waiting near the clinic entrance—Chloe Papadakis, standing with a nervous woman in a headscarf, clutching a small bag. Chloe waved as Aisha stepped out of her car, her face a mix of relief and uncertainty.

"Dr Khalid," Chloe greeted, her voice conveying tension. "This is Mrs. Ariana Bahar. She just moved to Cedar Valley, and… well, she was looking for someone she could trust." As Chloe introduced the patient to Aisha, she spoke urgently, "I found her in the park looking despondent and unwell. She speaks a little English. I convinced her to come here with me. I didn't know where else to go. I thought you'd know best how to help."

"Thank you, Chloe," replied Dr. Khalid. She and Ariana bow to each other, forgoing a handshake. "Please wait inside until we are finished in case we could use your help again."

Aisha's heart softened as she turned to the woman. She understood the bravery it took to come here, especially in a town grappling with undercurrents of suspicion. Offering a warm smile, she extended her hand. In Farsi, she said, "Mrs. Bahar, I'm Dr. Khalid. Please, come in. You're in safe hands here."

As she took Aisha's hand, the woman's face lit up hearing the familiar language. She glanced back at Chloe with a grateful nod before following Aisha into the clinic. Chloe followed as well, stopping in the lobby to wait.

In the lobby, Chloe found a hot water dispenser to make herself a cup of green hot tea. As she sipped her tea, she thought of the kindness she had shown by connecting the two Muslim women. She couldn't help but wonder what might have happened if Dr. Khalid was not Muslim and could not make Mrs. Bahar feel at ease. These thoughts troubled her, as she had become aware of the various challenges Muslims face in foreign countries, where they struggle to understand cultures that are vastly different from their own, and how her community worried about their own culture being diminished by the strangers' presence.

Chloe couldn't help but recognize the many health issues facing the refugees. These included challenges related to medications, dietary restrictions during Ramadan, family dynamics, gender preferences, attitudes and beliefs about health, misconceptions about the causes of certain diseases, and the complexities of navigating healthcare systems. All these challenges felt overwhelming to her and seemed far too complicated to contemplate, let alone manage. In her mind, Chloe concluded that Aisha would have a tough time.

Inside, as they moved to the exam room, Aisha sensed Mrs. Bahar's tension but kept her own manner calm, creating an atmosphere of safety and respect.

"Mrs. Bahar," Still speaking in Farsi, Aisha said softly once seated. "How have you been feeling?"

The woman hesitated, her fingers worrying the hem of her sleeve. "Doctor, I... I am fine. It's just ... things are difficult. My children, though they do not attend the local schools yet, ... they hear things that make them afraid."

Aisha's heart twisted. She understood all too well the weight of words that linger, unspoken but deeply felt, and the fear of being unwelcome in a place meant to be home. She reached out, covering Mrs. Bahar's hand with her own. "Your family is safe here. I'll do everything I can to make sure of it."

Mrs. Bahar nodded, her eyes shimmering with unshed tears, and Aisha felt her resolve harden. Cedar Valley's tension was more than words and glances; it was an invisible force permeating even the most vulnerable. While she had yet to see how it could be changed, she knew she couldn't stand idle.

After the appointment, as Aisha stepped out into the lobby, she saw Chloe lingering nearby, her expression thoughtful.

Mrs. Bahar emerged, bowing her head several times to express her gratitude to Chloe and Aisha. "*Shukran. Baraka Allahou feek*," said Ariana, meaning, "Thank you, God bless you."

Aisha quickly added, "Please take Mrs. Bahar through the pharmacy to collect her two medications," Aisha asked, looking directly at Chloe. "I have stressed to her to come for her next appointment in seven days, as indicated on the card."

"I will," Chloe replied, leading Mrs. Bahar out of the clinic.

Back in her office, Aisha closed her eyes briefly, gathering her thoughts. The quiet echo of Chloe's kindness towards Mrs Bahar warmed her heart. She was also encouraged by Teresa, at a recent appointment, to share about her unique history assignment, and her high school students were warming up to discussing and writing about their family's ancestors. These quiet kindnesses created a soft undercurrent of connection that felt fragile yet powerful. She vowed to be part of that light, however difficult the road ahead might be.

Early morning darkness wrapped around Dan Larson as he lay awake, thoughts running circles in his mind. Beside him, Rebecca stirred, sensing his unrest. They had both been awake for some time now, sharing the silence and the unspoken worries between them.

"What's going through that head of yours, Dan Larson?" Rebecca finally broke the silence, her voice soft.

Dan sighed, running a hand over his face. "A lot of things. It feels like there's a fire smoldering in Cedar Valley, and I don't know how to put it out. President Taylor told me to be a peacemaker, but sometimes, it feels like I'm standing in a field of dry grass about to be ignited, with only a single bucket of water."

Rebecca turned to him, her gaze steady. "Being a peacemaker doesn't mean you must do it all at once, Dan. Think about it—Jesus didn't fix the world in a day. He worked with one person at a time, one moment at a time."

Dan smiled faintly. "You always bring it back to the basics. I love that about you."

Rebecca's face softened. "It's one of the reasons you married me, right?" She took his hand, squeezing it gently. "Just keep showing up. You'll find the path."

Dan hesitated, then shared something he hadn't told her yet. "I gave George Khan a call yesterday. Asked him to come by my office. I've been trying to think of ways to help him, but I'm not sure he's ready for it. He's hurting, carrying a lot of baggage from his past."

Rebecca nodded thoughtfully. "You have a good heart, Dan. But you're not responsible for what George does with the chance you give him. Just make sure he knows he's welcome and valued."

"I also ran into Caleb Mercer," Dan continued. "He's in a rough spot, too. He's got this bitterness simmering under the surface—anger at the world, his life, and himself. I tried to talk to him, offer him a bit of support, but it's like trying to hold onto smoke."

Rebecca listened; her expression thoughtful. "Maybe that's just it, Dan. Maybe you're not meant to solve everything for them. Sometimes, just having someone to lean on, someone who sees you, is enough."

Dan stared at the ceiling, feeling the weight of her words. "I hope you're right, Rebecca. I really do."

Rebecca settled back down, resting her head against his shoulder. "You always say, 'Let's find a way,' I have faith God will show you the way."

A QUIET REFLECTION

The shadows in Cedar Valley loomed larger with every passing day, their weight felt in every interaction and unspoken thought. Yet, even in the darkest corners, glimmers of light began to break through. Teresa's determination to plant seeds of understanding in her students, Caleb's quiet grappling with bitterness and responsibility, and Maryam's steadfast courage amid hostility reflected a town struggling to find its way.

Amid the protests and misunderstandings, acts of quiet bravery began to emerge. Aisha's care for Mrs. Bahar transcended barriers of fear and suspicion, while Chloe's unexpected kindness reminded others of the power of small actions. Even Dan's resolve to guide George and Caleb showed a commitment to bridge divides one step at a time.

These connections, though tentative, carried the promise of growth. No matter how small, each act of kindness and determination created ripples that could one day become waves. Cedar Valley's fractures remained, but they were no longer insurmountable. In every choice to listen instead of judge, to reach out instead of retreat, a new foundation was being built—one brick, one step, one quiet act of hope at a time.

CHAPTER 4
RIPPLES OF REFLECTION

Chloe Papadakis sat cross-legged on her dorm room bed, the crisp sound of rustling paper filling the quiet space. The local newspaper lay spread out before her, headlines jumping out with words like "division," "tensions," and "protests." Each article seemed to echo the unrest that had taken root in Cedar Valley, painting a picture of a town grappling with forces feeling as unpredictable as they were powerful.

She traced her finger over one article about the arrival of Afghan refugees, her mind drifted to her conversation with Dr. Aisha Khalid earlier in the week. After she had taken Mrs. Bahar back to the old high school, she returned to the clinic to talk with Dr. Khalid about the refugees. She wondered how she could help her town's residents combat fear and frustration about the refugees. Finding and helping Mrs. Bahar put a human face on the strangers. The doctor's calm but firm words had planted a seed in Chloe, stirring within her a determination to understand the complexities of what was happening. For the first time, she felt a tug of responsibility—not just as a bystander, but as someone who could contribute to the changes needed in her community.

With a sigh, Chloe folded the paper and set it aside, her gaze shifting to the window where the last rays of sunlight painted the campus in shades of gold. *Maybe it was time to do more than just read about the issues,* she thought. *Maybe it was time to engage.*

Maryam Khan was busy behind the counter of her Deli, her thoughts distant as she prepared sandwiches for the lunch rush. Her encounter at the high school had left her shaken, a stark reminder of the resentment brewing in Cedar Valley. But she was determined not to let fear win. The refugees she'd helped that day reminded her of her family's journey, their challenges, and their courage to start anew.

A customer entered, and Maryam looked up, offering a warm smile despite her worries. She greeted them, her voice steady, finding comfort in the familiar rhythm of her work.

As she handed over the food, a fleeting memory of her homeland surfaced—a vivid image from her childhood when there was a lull in Pakistan's dangerous conflicts, so her parents brought the family to meet their grandparents. She saw the mountains, smelled the aroma of spices mingling with the fresh air, and marveled at the country's rich ancient history. She closed her eyes briefly, grounding herself in those memories, drawing strength from them.

"This is my home now," she thought. "I belong here, too."

With renewed resolve, she decided to continue her efforts, no matter how small, to bridge the divide growing around her. Maybe a kind word, a simple gesture, could make a difference. And if not, she would keep trying.

George Khan paced his small apartment, frustration etched across his face. The weight of his past, the whispers of "jailbird," seemed to follow him everywhere. He had tried to hold his head high, to rebuild, but the rejection felt relentless. Every closed door reminded him of a past he couldn't shake, no matter how hard he tried.

He reached for his phone, his hands trembling slightly as he considered calling his sister. She'd been his only lifeline in his youth, even into some of his prison years, until their father put a stop to it. She was the one person who tried so hard not to turn away. Yet, even if reconciliation with Maryam was possible, George knew he had to find his own way.

As he sank into his worn-out armchair, he murmured a quiet prayer, his voice filled with determination and despair. "Lord, show me the way," he whispered, closing his eyes against the flickering shadows on the walls. "I need something, anything, to hold onto."

In that stillness, he felt a flicker of hope—fragile, but present. It wasn't much, but it was enough to keep him going, to try again the next day.

Aisha returned to her clinic, her mind lingering on her earlier interactions. The uncertainty filling the town also seeped into her clinic, patients arriving with worried glances, unspoken fears hanging in the air.

She took a deep breath, steadying herself as she prepared for the day ahead. She knew her work had become more than just medicine; it was an act of compassion, a reminder to those who entered that they weren't alone. She moved from patient to patient, offering not just treatment but reassurance, a kind word here, a soft smile there. In an increasingly fractured world, these small gestures felt like anchors, holding her—and maybe her patients—steady against the rising tide of division.

The day stretched on, and with each interaction, Aisha found herself more determined to bring kindness into Cedar Valley, one person at a time.

Chloe returned to her dorm room later that night, her mind racing with thoughts of everything she had read and felt that day. As she glanced back at the newspaper, she noticed an op-ed calling for unity and understanding—a plea to the residents of Cedar Valley to see past their differences. The words resonated, filling her with a quiet determination to take action, no matter how small.

The following day, she found herself drawn to the voter registration table on campus, where bright posters and smiling faces of volunteers filled the space with an almost infectious energy. Voting had never seemed as important as it did now that she had read enough to know how leadership makes a significant difference in healing or further fracturing a community: with a steadying breath, she approached the table and filled out the volunteer form. As she returned it, a volunteer offered her a button with the slogan, "Be the Change." She pinned it on her jacket, feeling a quiet thrill of purpose. Not only had she done her civic duty by registering to vote as her father expected, but she was also going to help others do it.

As Chloe left, her steps felt lighter. For the first time, she felt like an observer and an active part of the town's story. Maybe she couldn't change everything on her own, but she could make her voice heard. And perhaps, in her small way, she could help Cedar Valley find its way back to unity. She also thought about how good it felt to help Mrs. Bahar. Maybe she could help more refugees and residents at Dr. Khalid's clinic. She quickened her step to go by the clinic before her next class.

Caleb Mercer had a sense of disquiet as he made his way down Main Street. His footsteps echoed in the early quiet, the dark storefronts reflecting his exhaustion and frustration back at him. Cedar Valley was changing, and each day, it felt more foreign.

He was met with a familiar voice as he rounded the corner near the bakery. "Caleb? That you?" Mr. Hamilton, a retired teacher, was sweeping the bakery steps, his slow, steady movements breaking the silence.

"Morning, Mr. Hamilton," Caleb replied, though he did not stop. The old man's gaze lingered, seeming to reach into the disquiet Caleb felt deeply.

"Long night?" Mr. Hamilton's voice held a knowing kindness.

Caleb shrugged, avoiding eye contact. "You could say that."

The old man sighed, resting the broom against his shoulder. "A lot of folks feel the same way lately. Town's changing, Caleb. People are changing."

Caleb nodded but did not respond. He felt the weight of the town's divisions pressing on him as he walked away.

After the confrontation by the old school, Caleb tried to wash away the anger and grime at a nearby gas station. He leaned over the sink, water pooling in his hands as he scrubbed his knuckles. His reflection stared back at him, haunted. He thought of his grandfather, a veteran, and his old stories about "foreigners" and how war had carved lines between "us" and "them."

Just as Caleb stepped outside, Dan Larson's car pulled up to a pump. Dan spotted him and called out, "Hey! Caleb! Wait up!"

"I'm busy," Caleb shouted back, determined to walk away.

Dan, undeterred, jogged over and caught his arm, dodging as Caleb instinctively swung his fist.

"Whoa!" Dan raised both hands in surrender, his eyes wide. "I just need a minute."

Further startled by the rough condition of Caleb's knuckles, Dan asked, "What happened?"

"What does it look like happened?" Caleb angrily retorted. "And no, I don't feel like talking about it!" He did not want to admit that one of his angry outbursts resulted in a physical altercation this time. On his way home, walking past the old high school, he observed a few men standing. He heard their angry conversation about not wanting the refugees in the town.

"We don't want these people here. Send them back to fix their own mess!" "Yes, they did not learn from our two decades of sacrifice that they were supposed to learn to fight for their own freedom."

Sick of the conflict, Caleb had run up on them, fists flying. "What do you know about sacrifice? You have no idea what those people have gone through!"

After landing a few punches, two guys trapped his arms, and the third drew back, his fist aimed for Caleb's abdomen. Suddenly, in the fading light, they recognized each other. They were all work acquaintances from the closed factory. The one lowering his fist had served in the military like Caleb. The four stood back from each other, catching their breath.

The army veteran's face was stricken with grief. "Caleb! You know how many buddies I lost over there, mostly because of villagers betraying us! One of our interpreters even led us into an ambush; we had heavy casualties! You know our sacrifice was for nothing! We just handed it all back to the Taliban and left them all our equipment! Now you are taking their side?!" He angrily threw his fist towards the school building. The two men stared at each other. Their agony was stark in their unshed tears, their broken souls hiding just behind. Caleb hung his head, then reached out his hand. They shook hands, shared a brief hug of combat brothers, and walked away in different directions.

Caleb took a steadying breath. "You want to help, Dan? Then talk to them," he pointed toward the school, "the people inside. They're not the enemy. They're human beings, families, just as lost as we are. We can't 'fix' our town's tension by keeping them at a distance."

Dan frowned, absorbing Caleb's words. "I don't know what to say, Caleb. I don't want to keep at a distance; I don't know how to approach them. I don't even speak Afghan."

"Afghan isn't a language." Caleb's voice was edged with frustration. He paused, gathering his thoughts. "Maybe you should start by learning who they are. Talk to the people who brought them here—ask them for an interpreter so you can talk to them. Then, you can ask the refugees questions. What are their names? What did they do before they got here? I'm sure they are not all interpreters the military evacuated with their families. What do they need now? How can we make them comfortable with us reaching out?"

Dan nodded slowly. "Alright, that makes sense. But where do I start?"

Caleb met his gaze. "Read up on their culture, Dan. Find out what commonalities our community can offer them to help them feel welcome. How can we build on those commonalities between our cultures so our townspeople feel better about the changes happening? Ask yourself what it's like to be them. If you really want to be a peacemaker, it will take more than good intentions; it will take good actions, too."

Dan's expression softened. "You're right, Caleb. I have wanted to help them since they arrived. Will you help me learn how? I can't do it alone." For the first time, Caleb saw a flicker of sincerity, a willingness to listen. He gave a brief nod. "Alright, Dan. But remember, it's about respect. These people need to feel like they belong here as much as we do."

The two men stood in the twilight, the weight of Cedar Valley's tensions between them. It was a small bridge for now, but it was something to build on.

Avery Sullivan sat rigidly in the small, overly lit conference room, feeling the chill of the polished surface beneath her hands. The school board table gleamed under fluorescent lights, creating a harsh glare that seemed to amplify the scrutiny of the board members across from her. Expressions ranged from skeptical to dismissive, each gaze carrying its unspoken challenge. Beside her, Teresa Nikas glanced at the notes they'd carefully prepared, her fingers tapping an anxious rhythm on the pages. They had walked into this room armed with words, determined to defend a project they believed in—a simple assignment to help students explore their family histories. But now, after an anonymous objection to the project, it felt as if they were standing trial.

Avery took a steadying breath, knowing the weight of this conversation went beyond the assignment. "We're not asking for anything radical," she began, keeping her tone as calm as she could. "All we're trying to do is give students a space to reflect on their heritage, to find common ground in a town that's..." She hesitated, feeling the palpable resistance in the room closing in. "...increasingly divided."

The board members shifted, a few leaning back in their chairs with arms crossed, signaling doubt. Chairman Ron Freeman smoothed his silver tie with an air of practiced patience. He leaned forward, his voice calm but firm. "Ms. Sullivan, while we appreciate your intentions, we must consider the parents' concerns. Bringing up these... cultural backgrounds might stir up more tension than it resolves."

Teresa's eyes flashed with frustration, and before she could hold back, she interjected, "The tension is already here," her voice edged with a firmness she could not mask. "We see it every day in the classrooms. Ignoring it won't make it disappear."

A heavy silence settled over the room, and Avery felt a flicker of doubt rise within her. She had known, they both had known, that this would be an uphill battle, but facing the board's scrutinizing gaze made the path forward feel steeper than ever. Yet, as she glanced at Teresa, she drew strength from her friend's unyielding resolve. They could not back down—not now. This wasn't merely about an assignment; it was about giving their students, and perhaps the town itself, a chance to heal, to find a sliver of unity amidst the division.

Avery adjusted her notes, her mind racing for the right words. She thought of her students, their diverse faces, the stories waiting to be heard. "We want our students to know that their stories matter. That their families, their histories, have value. If we silence that part of them, we're missing an opportunity to build understanding."

The board members exchanged glances, some softening, others unmoved. Finally, the man in the silver tie sighed, his gaze settling on her with a look that was more weary than adversarial. "We'll take it under consideration," he said, his tone carrying the weight of bureaucratic indifference.

As Avery and Teresa gathered their papers and left the room, they exchanged a look—a shared understanding that, while they might not have won the board over entirely, they had at least voiced the importance of this effort.

Lars Olson spent his morning in the quiet solitude of his hardware store, reflecting on recent changes in Cedar Valley. Once a bustling hub for the community, the store had become an eerily silent reminder of how much things had shifted. He thought about the past, the friendly faces, the camaraderie that once filled these aisles. Even Dan, who used to come by for a chat now and then, had recently taken on the same in-and-out routine as everyone else, buying what he needed without lingering.

Trying to shake off the melancholy, Lars busied himself by organizing a display of tools near the front window, his mind drifting through memories of better times. He wondered how many others besides him and Caleb felt the strange unease seeping through the town. Was it only Caleb trying to hold onto an idealized past, or did hope fuel others' fear and anger? Would Cedar Valley see better times again?

As the morning wore on, not a single customer walked through the door. Lars glanced at the clock, feeling an unfamiliar hollowness. The store, usually a steady stream of faces and subdued voices, seemed abandoned. He was actually starting to feel physically ill about it. In a very uncharacteristic action for him, he left his senior employee in charge and went home. It wasn't until later that he learned about Caleb's chaos at the old high school.

☐ A QUIET REFLECTION

In the ripples of reflection spreading through Cedar Valley, each individual faced a choice: to retreat further into isolation or to step forward, however tentatively, toward understanding. Chloe's decision to engage rather than observe marked a turning point, a shift from uncertainty to action. Her quiet determination reflected the possibilities that emerged when fear was met with curiosity.

While grappling with rejection and hostility, Maryam and George found strength in their memories and faith, drawing on these anchors to face an uncertain future. Caleb's blunt honesty challenged Dan to rethink his approach, bridging a gap that had seemed insurmountable. Meanwhile, Teresa and Avery's resolve to foster dialogue in the classroom embodied the courage required to address division head-on despite resistance.

Though small, the echoes of these efforts carried the potential to grow into something greater. In their collective reflections and choices, the people of Cedar Valley began to plant the seeds of a community not yet whole but undeniably resilient. The path forward remained steep, but the town found flickers of light breaking through the shadows in each gesture of kindness and determination.

CHAPTER 5
ECHOES OF BELONGING

Maryam Khan walked slowly down Cedar Valley's Main Street, her thoughts drifting like the crisp autumn leaves that lined her path. She knew, despite everything, that she was blessed. All nations and neighborhoods wrestled with their conflicts; she had seen that much in her life. But the difference between Cedar Valley and her homeland of Pakistan ran deep, like an underground river with its quiet current. In Pakistan, your family name, faith, and birthplace often determine who you are allowed to be. It was as though the path was already chosen, each step placed carefully within invisible boundaries. In America, and especially in this quiet town, freedom was woven into everything—even in times of hardship.

Yet, as she glanced around, noting the tight expressions and wary looks exchanged by neighbors who once greeted each other warmly, Maryam felt the sting of something familiar. It reminded her of the closed doors her parents told her and her siblings about that they faced when they were in Pakistan. Especially once it was known they were Christians. They escaped because they wanted a better, safer future for their children. There was an ache in her chest as she saw Cedar Valley veering toward that same coldness they suffered when they first opened the Deli. She wondered if her neighbors felt the same.

"Morning, Maryam," a familiar voice called, drawing her back to the moment. It was Lars Olson, sweeping the sidewalk in front of his hardware store.

Maryam offered a warm smile. "Good morning, Lars. How's business?"

"Not bad," Lars replied, his voice as steady as the rhythm of his broom. "Though these days, seems like folks would rather furtively murmur, and complain than shop. Guess everyone's got an opinion about what's happening."

Maryam nodded, feeling the weight of unspoken words between them. "It's the same in any community, Lars. People are on edge, and sometimes talking feels like the only way to understand things."

Lars paused, looking at her thoughtfully. "Your family's seen a lot more than most of us, haven't you?"

She gave a small laugh, more out of habit than humor. "In Pakistan, conflict was something my parents lived with daily, but hope—hope was what kept them moving forward to make it out to a better life for us kids. That same spirit exists here, but we're all struggling to hold onto it."

Lars nodded, his expression softening. "We'll get through it. People just need time."

As she walked on, Maryam felt a renewed sense of purpose. Perhaps she could remind her neighbors of what they shared amidst Cedar Valley's confusion and strife.

The early morning air was crisp as George walked down the empty street; his hands jammed deep in his coat pockets. He had dressed carefully that morning, smoothing his worn but clean clothes, brushing his hair, and even shaving. He'd left his efficiency apartment with a spark of expectation headed for his meeting with Dan. He hoped against hope that Dan had a lead on a job for him. He could not think of why else Dan would ask him to his office for a meeting.. The walk was quiet, and he chose a longer route, letting his mind wander through Cedar Valley's familiar streets, which had once felt like home.

Passing through the park, George noticed Caleb sitting alone on a bench, nursing the remnants of last night's frustrations. Knowing Caleb's quick temper and unpredictable moods, George hesitated before calling out. "Hi, Caleb, what's up?"

Caleb did not look up at first, his hands buried deep in his coat, his shoulders hunched against the world. Eventually, George sighed. "Why are you so deep in thought, Caleb? I called your name twice before you even noticed."

Caleb shrugged, a bitter edge to his tone. "Little Lady nagged me out of the house. Again. Seems like it's becoming a habit."

"That's rough. At least I don't have that kind of problem." George tried to lighten the conversation but sensed the weariness that clung to Caleb's words.

"So I'm just sitting here thinking about this town and all its problems. About everything, really. There was a brief silence before Caleb asked, "What about you? What's got you out here so early? Where are you headed?"

"Dan wanted to meet up. Says he's got something to talk about," George replied, his voice cautious but hopeful.

Caleb gave a short laugh. "Oh, he tried that with me too. Tells me life can be better. I'm not falling for that naive optimism. Look around, George. Everyone's complaining, but nobody's actually doing anything to make things better.

George placed a hand on Caleb's shoulder, a small gesture of solidarity. "He means well, Caleb. I think he genuinely believes things can change."

Caleb glanced at him, a shadow of skepticism clouding his eyes. But after a pause, he softened slightly. "I know he does." Changing the subject, he said, "Listen, George. Remember I told you about a job lead I had from an old army buddy? Ben has some work on the side, nothing big, but it's something. He asked if I wanted in, but honestly... I told him you could probably use it more than me."

The words caught George by surprise. He had gotten used to people looking past him or avoiding his gaze. "Why'd you turn it down?"

Caleb shrugged again, looking away as if the answer were written in the trees. "Don't know. Maybe I just figured it might mean more to you right now. Besides," he added, with a reluctant half-smile, "I need to hone my people skills before I can cooperate properly in a work setting again. So says my wife anyway."

George felt a flicker of warmth, smiling at the comment. "Thanks, Caleb. I don't know what to say."

"Don't say anything," Caleb replied quickly, brushing off the sentiment. "Ben's a good guy. He'll look out for you if you show him you're worth it."

"Well, I'll take what I can get." George hesitated. "Listen... I'm grateful. Not many people are willing to look out for a guy like me."

Caleb gave him a quick nod. "Just keep it quiet. I got a reputation to uphold."

With that, George chuckled softly, sensing the rough camaraderie between them. "I hear you. Well, I better keep moving. Don't want to keep Dan waiting."

As George started to walk away, he turned back with a parting reminder. "Take care of yourself, Caleb. And remember, Jesus loves you and me."

Caleb scoffed but managed a faint smile. "Yeah, yeah, I know that. Good luck, George."

George's steps were lighter as he left his afternoon meeting with Ben. The news he received had filled him with a kind of hope he hadn't felt in years. Ben offered him intermittent small jobs—work that was not permanent but was somewhat steady, something George could build on. Ben also mentioned that Caleb had turned down the job first, insisting George needed it more. Again, the sacrifice struck George deeply, and as he walked back to his apartment, he felt a shift in his heart, a softening of the resentment that had built up over the years.

Back in his apartment, George pulled out his phone and dialed Caleb's number, feeling gratitude replacing the usual tension in his voice. When Caleb picked up, his tone was gruff as always, but George sensed a faint openness. "Hey, Caleb. Just wanted to thank you for the job lead. I… I really appreciate it."

Caleb's voice softened almost imperceptibly. "How'd it go?"

George took a breath, letting the words sink in. "I got it. Thanks to you. Can't tell you what it means, knowing you thought of me first. You and Ben… you've given me a glimmer of hope. That's more than I've had in a long time."

A muffled noise came through the line, Caleb's voice breaking the moment. "Hey, I gotta go. Things are getting heated over by the old school. Looks like trouble."

George felt a familiar unease tighten his stomach. "Be careful, Caleb," he said, but the line had already gone dead.

As he pocketed his phone, the lingering words from his talk with Dan echoed in his mind—a call to step up, to take ownership of his place in Cedar Valley. For the first time in a long while, George felt he had a role to play, a reason to stand tall. Dan's faith in him had been palpable, a rare gift now weighing heavily on his heart that failure was not an option. He resolved not to let Dan's, or Ben's trust in him go to waste. Then, the call with Caleb served as a reminder of the unrest brewing in town, and George couldn't shake the feeling that, somehow, his actions mattered now more than ever.

Chloe tightened her scarf as she stepped onto the chilly street, her gaze drifting over Cedar Valley's quiet morning. The town was still waking up, its buildings softened by the early light. Chloe's mind was occupied with thoughts of the gathering she was about to attend—a gathering more than a meeting, a place for sharing and, maybe, understanding.

She pulled her jacket closer as she approached the small café where a few familiar faces had already gathered. Inside, the warmth of friendly conversation greeted her, mingling with the comforting scent of coffee and freshly baked goods. Avery waved from a table near the back, her face lighting up as Chloe joined her.

"Glad you made it," Avery said, her voice steady but carrying an undertone of weariness. Chloe could tell the town's recent tensions had worn on her. Despite that, Avery's presence felt like an anchor for which Chloe found herself grateful. Ms. Sullivan was a popular teacher at her high school, so she felt assurance being with her.

Around them, a handful of others gathered in quiet clusters, their conversations hushed yet laced with anticipation. Chloe noticed a few of her mother's friends exchanging concerned looks. Some spoke in whispers, mentioning the newcomers— "the visitors," they called them— who'd brought gratitude and uncertainty with them. Chloe's mind turned to the refugees she'd been helping at the clinic since she found Mrs. Bahar despondent in the park. Many had warmth in their eyes despite everything they'd been through.

"They feel so isolated," Chloe murmured, more to herself than anyone else. Avery glanced at her, nodding thoughtfully.

"You're right," Avery said. "And I can't help but think… maybe we're not doing enough to help them feel welcomed."

Chloe felt a surge of purpose rise within her, a determination that felt old and new. "My mother always says it's not enough to be kind from a distance. You have to step into their world, even when it's uncomfortable. That's why I had to help Mrs. Bahar, which led me to help regularly in Dr. Khalid's clinic."

The words settled between them, and Chloe saw the hint of a smile on Avery's face—a quiet acknowledgment of the truth in her statement.

As the room grew quiet, Caleb entered, his expression guarded but not unkind. He nodded to a few familiar faces before making his way to an empty seat nearby. Chloe watched him, sensing the weight he carried—the kind of burden that pressed on a person, making them feel both part of the community and somehow set apart from it.

"They don't see it, do they?" Caleb said after a moment, almost to himself. Avery turned, meeting his gaze. "The refugees, I mean. They don't see how the town's attitude isn't personal against them—it's fear of the change they bring to our home."

Avery thought about the layers of fear and misunderstanding that seemed to tangle up in so many interactions between the residents and the new arrivals. "Fear or something deeper?" she asked. "I think some people are afraid of what they don't understand… or what reminds them of parts of themselves they'd rather forget."

Caleb glanced away; his face softened in quiet thought. The conversations around them continued, punctuated by nods and brief moments of silence as people took in the complexity of what they were sharing. At that moment, Avery felt a shift—a small, fragile movement towards something better.

In a quieter part of the room, Teresa sat with a notebook open in front of her, scribbling down thoughts. Her gaze occasionally swept over the gathering, and Avery caught the faintest look of hope in her eyes, tempered with the cautious optimism of someone who knew too well the pain of broken expectations.

Avery watched as Lars entered the café, his presence solid and un-hurried. He stopped to greet a few neighbors, exchanging brief words before making his way over to join Teresa. Together, they began to discuss the ways they might encourage more of the town to participate in understanding and supporting the refugees—no grand gestures, just small, meaningful ways to show that they cared.

Avery felt a sense of unity, a quiet resolve weaving through the room. These were her friends, her neighbors, and people who cared enough to listen and start taking small steps. Chloe was having similar thoughts. She needed to muster the courage not only to work at the voter registration table, but also to actively educate students about opportunities to help the refugees. And even if Cedar Valley still held its divisions, maybe today, they were beginning to bridge them. Dan and Rebecca Larson entered the room, and the meeting began.

Dan Larson stood on the corner of Main Street, waiting for Lars Olson, who approached from his hardware store, a thoughtful look etched on his face. They greeted each other with a firm handshake, the kind exchanged by men who respected each other's dedication to the community. As they spoke, Rebecca came down the sidewalk, her face lit with a bright, welcoming smile that softened the crisp autumn air.

"Hey there!" Dan said, noticing her radiant expression. "What's got you in such high spirits?"

Rebecca looked between her husband and Lars, unable to contain her enthusiasm. "I just came from helping with the relief efforts we planned at the Café, then we organized at our church. Latter-Day Saints Charities just delivered the refugees' essentials—food, clothing, hygiene supplies, to name a few. You should have seen their faces, Dan. The children were laughing when they were given a handful of candy, a ball, and coloring books with crayons. The men grateful for warm jackets, and the women found comfort in the familiar styles and colors of the clothing. It was amazing to meet them. A couple named Alim and Padam stepped up to speak for their community."."

"That's wonderful to hear, Rebecca," Lars said, stepping aside slightly, respectfully as she joined their conversation. "It must have meant the world to them. Your church truly shows compassion."

Dan nodded in agreement. "That's exactly what we hope to do, Lars. It's not just us, though. It's you and the community. This donation drive we planned at our meeting came together because of all of us. It's why we give our tithes and contribute to these causes. It's important, especially now."

Lars' gaze softened, and he replied with quiet conviction. "These efforts show that Cedar Valley is, at its core, a place of compassion. Your church is a beacon of hope, especially in these times. The refugees will know we, as a community, care about them."

Rebecca continued, her eyes shining with purpose. "I believe this will do more than meet their needs; it might inspire others in town to reach out. Small acts can be contagious."

Lars nodded thoughtfully, adding, "Perhaps it will help ease some unease here. Faith can work wonders in calming fears. Our churches can bring people together in ways few other things can. I think, however, Cedar Valley residents are worried we are neglecting our own. We need to be sure that is not happening."

Dan nodded his head in agreement. But inspired by the three's shared conviction about meeting the refugees' needs, he continued, "If more people understood the value of such outreach, maybe they'd see the refugees differently—as part of the community, just like the rest of us."

Rebecca touched his arm gently. "That's why we continue giving, Dan. It's more than a duty—a privilege to help someone feel they belong."

They stood there, united by a sense of purpose and mutual respect, each understanding the importance of building bridges in Cedar Valley. It was a moment of quiet solidarity, an example of the small yet powerful connections beginning to heal the divisions in their town.

The gathering had come together almost by word of mouth—a spontaneous response to the growing tensions in Cedar Valley. Avery and Teresa had spread the word, reaching out to those they knew shared a deep love for the town and a desire to understand the newcomers better. They had not wanted an official town hall meeting, which felt too formal, too stiff for what they hoped to accomplish. Instead, they had gathered in Maryam's Deli after hours, where everyone felt comfortable enough to speak freely, as friends more than as citizens with competing interests.

Avery looked around, feeling a mix of anticipation and nervousness. She had not expected such a turnout or anticipated how many would feel called to gather like this to bridge the widening gaps every day. This wasn't a town hall but a circle of friends, neighbors, and perhaps soon-to-be allies, each carrying their own stories, hopes, concerns, and hesitations.

The gathering was a mixed group, a blend of familiar faces and a few who usually avoided official town meetings. Chairs scraped against the wooden floor as people settled in, murmurs filling the room. Teresa glanced around, her hands clasped tightly, her nerves barely hidden behind a calm expression. She hadn't expected such a large turnout.

The atmosphere was thick with curiosity and a cautious willingness to listen. They had all come with opinions and assumptions, no doubt, but there was also a hope that something meaningful might emerge from this gathering. As the room quieted, Teresa cleared her throat, sensing the importance of this moment. Just as she was about to speak, she caught sight of Maryam, who had raised her hand.

"Maryam," Teresa said, offering a nod of acknowledgment.

Maryam stood, looking around the room. Her expression held a vulnerability new to the town's usually assured deli owner. "I wanted to share something," she began, her voice steady but soft. "I've been bringing food to the refugees at the school, and... well, it's been an experience that's changed how I see things."

People turned their attention to her, some with curiosity, others with folded arms and guarded expressions.

"These families—parents, children, elders—they're scared," she continued, choosing her words carefully. "Not just of the journey they've been through, but of us. They saw what happened to me when the angry crowd was in front of the old high school when I was knocked down. They know many don't want them here. They see the same looks we've all seen, people watching them at the clinic or in the park when they venture out of the school. The cautious glances and suspected anger simmering beneath polite words. They feel it, too."

A few heads turned down as if acknowledging the truth of her words. Maryam took a steadying breath, gathering her courage to press on. "You know, it wasn't so different when my family came here years ago. We faced our struggles and our moments of doubt. It took time to feel like we belonged."

Teresa caught Aisha's gaze from across the room, and she nodded in silent encouragement. Taking that as a signal, Aisha stood beside Maryam, gently touching her arm.

"I know exactly what you're talking about," Aisha began, her calm, compassionate voice filling the room. "When I first moved to Cedar Valley, I was welcomed by some, yes, but there were moments...moments when I felt like an outsider in my new hometown." She paused, scanning the crowd, letting her words settle. "I understand what these families are feeling—the loneliness, the fear, the uncertainty. And I can tell you this: the small gestures, the quiet moments of kindness, make the biggest difference."

She glanced at Maryam, who nodded in solidarity.

A few people shifted in their seats, visibly moved by Aisha's words. Sitting near the back, Lars Olson raised his hand, catching Teresa's attention. "I get what you're saying, Dr. Khalid, I really do," he said, his voice thoughtful. "But it's hard for people to get past their worries. They've got families to provide for and protect. City resources, like those of community and church charities, are stretched beyond their limits. Losing factory jobs economically crippled so many of our families. We have to make sure we take care of our own as well. Plus, we've all heard about the clashes between cultures in other towns. How can we be sure that won't happen here?"

Aisha met Lars's gaze with calm assurance. "I understand those worries too, Lars. But fear often grows when there's a lack of understanding. When we don't take the time to know each other." She gestured around the room. "We're all here tonight because we care about Cedar Valley. Imagine if we extended that care to those who've come seeking refuge. Imagine seeing them as people with stories, just like we have."

Caleb, who had been quietly observing, finally spoke up. "I've spent time overseas—Afghanistan, Iraq. I've seen what happens when we don't try to bridge these divides." His voice had an edge to it, shaped by the weight of experience. "These folks didn't ask to be uprooted from their homes. They didn't plan on starting over here any more than we planned to host them. As Lars said, we already had serious challenges before they got here. We are all fearful that there are not enough resources to go around. But that's where we are."

He paused, glancing across the attendees, seeing they were listening intently. "They're here now. And they're just as lost, maybe even more so, than we are."

George was standing just outside the Deli, partially hidden by the soda dispenser, where he was not noticed. Nodding slowly to himself, he knew this was one of the opportunities Dan had encouraged him to watch for to regain his place in Cedar Valley. He bravely stepped into the room, saying, "I know how they feel, losing everything. Family, friends, freedom, forgiveness, including forgiving myself. While it was my poor choices that I lost everything," his voice broke. He cleared his throat and continued. "These families had brave family members who worked with our military against the Taliban's cruel control. When our government pulled out so shamefully, they doomed these families to fleeing or probable certain death. They are scared. I am, too. How to start over, making a life in a strange world. I am in a strange world with them. Both rejected by this community, knowing most of its residents want them gone." Not wanting to see the group's reaction to his heartfelt honesty, he quickly left, almost running down the street to get away.

Chloe lingered near the back of the packed deli. She clutched the notebook she'd brought, the corners of its pages bent from her nervous fiddling. She had written a few notes, intending to voice her thoughts if the opportunity arose. But now, standing among a sea of confident voices, her own words felt small and inadequate.

She scanned the room, spotting Teresa Nikas, her former high school teacher, standing with Avery Sullivan. Both women nodded encouragingly. Chloe felt a pang of envy—they always seemed to know what to say and how to say it.

Her notebook remained closed. *"Why can't I just say something?"* she whispered to herself. *"Anything."*

The room was quiet, each person weighing the shared pain and resilience woven through the speakers' words. George's input, however, took them all by surprise. Especially Maryam. She sat very still in shock, not having seen him in so many years, not even seeking him out once he was released. Tears flowed as she dropped her face into her hands and quietly sobbed; she knew the truth of her brother's words – he had been abandoned. As for the townspeople, they did ignore him, refuse to give him any chances, except for Dan, Lars, Caleb, and Caleb's buddy Ben, the rest of them acted like he did not exist. At that moment, the fear and judgment that had bound the room together seemed to loosen just a little, giving way to something softer—a fragile empathy, even for George.

Teresa finally spoke, her voice steady with newfound purpose. "Maybe that's our answer," she said. "To lean into that empathy, to take small steps, as Maryam and Dr. Khalid have done. To show these families they are not alone."

The room was silent as the words settled over them, the tiny embers of hope igniting in hearts that, just moments before, had felt closed and cautious. It wasn't a solution to every problem Cedar Valley faced, but as they looked around at each other, they could sense that it was a beginning.

Dusk settled over Cedar Valley, casting a golden hue through the high windows into the church hall. Inside, quiet murmurs of gathered neighbors filled the room, a mix of familiar faces both anxious and resolute. What had started as scattered conversations across the town had woven together, leading to this—a collective breath of curiosity and unspoken hope.

Dan Larson, steady as ever, stood by the doorway, nodding to each person as they trickled in. Avery and Teresa took seats toward the front, their hands busy with papers holding nothing more than notes on possible solutions. For many in the room, just coming together like this was a victory—a tentative acknowledgment that their shared unease had a common thread.

Dan looked at Lars Olson, who stood nearby with a pensive expression, his arms crossed as if weighing each thought before it surfaced. Lars had voiced what many others were thinking: the arrival of the Afghan refugees wasn't just a logistical concern; it stirred questions about the town's identity, shared values, and resilience.

Despite being cold outside, the church hall was warm and muggy, as more than one hundred people crowded in. Every folding chair was taken. Some people sat on benches near the side walls, and others stood in the back. In one corner, Teresa Nikas had set up a long folding table filled with cookies, coffee, water, and sweet tea. A few people lingered near the table as if trying to look unconcerned about the meeting that was about to take place.

Dan Larson stood at the front of the room on a small stage used for special events. He wore a navy suit, white shirt, and blue tie. He looked more like a politician than a building contractor or preacher; tonight, he was a combination of those people. These were his people, whether or not they went to his church. This was his town, his home, and his challenge to reunite them.

He looked up as Caleb Mercer slipped in through the side door. Dan nodded at Caleb and motioned him forward. Caleb, his head bent low as if not seeing others meant they couldn't see him, approached the stage with his arms folded across his chest.

"Please," said Dan. "You don't have to say anything if you don't want to. Just back me up. After all, it was your idea."

"Our idea," Caleb murmured. He took his place, leaning against the wall behind Dan.

The crowd began to quiet.

"Ladies and gentlemen," Dan began.

"Only them?" someone joked from the back of the room.

Dan smiled. "Citizens of Cedar Valley."

"Oh, hell," said the same man. "And here I thought we were gonna have some fun."

A titter of laughter worked its way across the room until someone else yelled, "Give it a rest, Joe!"

The crowd quieted, and Dan began again. "We have a problem in this town that should have been addressed long before now. There is a saying, if you don't face your fears as soon as possible, they grow in your head until they become bigger than any threat that actually exists. What we have here is a lot of fear in the face of no threat at all, at least not from the refugees who have been sent here.

"They should go back where they came from!" Someone yelled.

Dan shielded his eyes against the bright overhead lights to find the speaker. He couldn't. He diverted from his prepared remarks. "They can't. As you know, the United States pulled out of Afghanistan suddenly, leaving behind many people who had helped us maintain peace in that country. Some of these people—many of them—were interpreters. Many were left behind and killed for helping us. A few escaped, leaving friends, family, and loved ones behind, some who were punished in their stead.

"So, why don't they go somewhere else?" someone asked. The question may have seemed brutal, but his tone was level, inquiring, with an honesty that many people shared.

"They have nowhere to go," Dan explained. "They were brought here by the federal government, and until something changes, this is where they will stay." Dan paused a few minutes to let his words sink in.

The person asking the question took a step back and scowled.

"My wife, Rebecca, and Maryam have been bringing them essentials. Dr Khalid has been treating them in the clinic. They want to be part of this community." Dan added.

Another man, seated in front, raised his hand to speak.

"Yes," said Dan.

He stood. "Are you asking this community of good Christian folks to allow Muslims to set up a mosque here? What about our children? Will these guys try to convert them? What then? We were at war with the Taliban. They ruled Afghanistan. I want to agree with you, but the whole thing makes me—makes us nervous." He glanced at his wife, who nodded as he sat down.

A few people murmured amongst themselves. Caleb opened his mouth to speak and then shut it again. He didn't want to lose his temper.

"You're right, of course," Dan said, although he did not agree in his heart. Somewhere in his background, he had learned to launch an opposition with a compliment. "Most people in this town are good Christians, but others are good Muslims; some are good Greek Orthodites." He stumbled over his concocted word. "Still others are atheists and agnostics and Catholics."

"That's as good as being atheist," someone said sarcastically.

Dan did his best to ignore the comment and not roll his eyes. "What I'm trying to say is that what holds us together as a community is not how we worship God but how we treat each other. We are good people. Whatever you believe, you also believe that your neighbors mean well, care about the town and its children, and want peace and normalcy back in their lives. He took a deep breath and glanced at Caleb, who remained quiet. Dan turned back to the crowd. "We all want to go back to having normal lives, and so do our visitors, I mean new neighbors." He deliberately avoided the word 'aliens.' "They are as afraid of us as we are of them."

Both Dr. Aisha Khalid and Maryam Khan stood up. Aisha spoke for both of them. "We agree," she said. "When I first came here many years ago, I was frightened. I don't know how I would have survived if it hadn't been for Maryam befriending me. She introduced me to so many nice and caring people. Eventually, I felt welcomed." She turned for a moment to address those around her. "Maryam and I do not share the same religion."

People looked at each other in surprise.

"Nor are we from Afghanistan."

Again, more looks.

"Maryam and I are both from Pakistan. It is a very different country, even though it has much in common with Afghanistan. It would be like the United States and Canada. We are cousins—the kind of cousins who occasionally get angry and fight each other. Maryam is also a Christian...." Aisha stopped and swallowed. Her hands trembled, betraying her nervousness. "I, on the other hand, am a Muslim."

Murmurs drifted past Aisha like the wind before a storm, but as she looked around the room, she saw other people smiling and nodding. They knew, of course, and they had accepted her without a word. She straightened her back, encouraged by their presence. "I am more than that. I am a doctor, but, more importantly, I am a mother. My son goes to school with your children. Sometimes, he is harassed for his faith or, the color of his skin, or the way he acts or dresses. We don't let it bother us much. As they say, children will be children." She turned back to Dan. "But we, we are not children. We are adults. We should know better than being afraid of those different from us."

Maryam sat down and tugged Aisha's sleeve to join her.

"One more thing, I just want to say that I agree with you, Mr. Larson. It's time we got to know our new neighbors." Aisha sat down.

Maryam squeezed her friend's hand.

Avery Sullivan then stood and waited to be recognized. Dan nodded to her.

"As you know, I've been teaching at the school for a few years now, and I know how nervous some kids are about what is happening in this town. They are not afraid of the—the—" She struggled to remember the word that Dan had used. "Visitors," she finally said. "They are afraid of us, of the arguing, of the tension, of the idea of what might happen if we don't figure this out. Our children need us to show them how to manage changes in our community with kindness and fairness. I tried discussing this with the school board. I had an idea for a project, but they are hesitant...."

"Hostile," Teresa Nikas 'whispered' just loud enough for everyone to hear in the back of the room. She bit into her third cookie.

"Hesitant to let it continue because a couple of parents complained.," Avery finished.

"What is it?" asked Lars.

"Except for the indigenous, and even they came from somewhere else a long time ago, we all came from somewhere," Avery said. "We all have ancestors or relatives who came from somewhere else." She glanced at the side door, seeing the school board chairman, Ron Freeman, leaning and chewing on beef jerky. She acknowledged him with a nod.

He kept chewing.

"I thought it would help the kids to understand this situation if they could study their history and find out where their ancestors came from and how they got here." She felt the eyes of people burning into her back. She sat down.

"Great idea," said someone, without sarcasm. "But why are you holding this meeting? Why isn't the town council doing this? What do they think?"

Mr Freeman finished his jerky and abruptly left.

Dan pursed his lips as he weighed his words. "The council has been discussing this matter," he said. He was pushing the truth a little. Mostly, it seemed, the council members were discussing how NOT to discuss it. "Some of them approached me to see if I could help." He glanced behind him again. "And I asked Caleb." Dan turned back to the crowd. "Caleb was stationed in Afghanistan for a while. He knows some of the language and is familiar with what happened there. He has agreed," Dan coughed, choking on the exaggerated word, "to approach them and try to set up a meeting between their community leaders and those of ours who are willing to talk with them." He glanced at the now empty doorway.

"A brief meeting to break the ice, so to speak. We need to find a way to work together, we can get past this and back to our normal lives."

"Is that true, Caleb?" asked Lars.

Caleb nodded but did not speak. It was not so much that he had agreed to the idea as he had let Dan strong-arm him into it. Still, he thought it was worth a shot.

Aisha stood up again. "If you need help," she started.

Maryam also stood up. "As you know, I've taken food there. I've befriended a few people. I can help, too."

"And me," said Lars, joining the others in standing.

"And me."

"And me."

"And me."

The volunteers were scattered around the room. For a few minutes, at least, Dan let the tension drain from his shoulders. "Great. I'd like to set up a meeting on Saturday for any volunteers. We can meet here around—" He thought for a second. "How does 10 a.m. sound?"

People nodded their heads.

Joe sputtered.

"You have something else to add?" Dan frowned.

"It's the road to hell, you know," said Joe. "All paved and that. You get my drift." He wandered outside and lit a cigarette.

"Ten, it is, then," said Dan.

"Can you let us all know what will happen next?" Teresa called out from her cookie table at the back of the room. She was now on cookie eight.

"Will do!" Dan answered back. "Anyone who wants to be updated, please leave your email address with Teresa."

Fifteen minutes later, the crowd had cleared except for Aisha, Lars, Avery, Caleb, Maryam, and Dan. Joe wandered back in as they discussed the next day's meeting.

"Okay, okay," said Joe. "If you're gonna do this futile thing, I'm in."

Dan Larson grinned.

Dan approached Caleb and placed a hand on his shoulder. "Thank you for coming," he said quietly.

Caleb gave a slight nod. "It's going to take time, Dan. But…I think we can make it work."

Dan offered a faint smile, his eyes reflecting the shared uncertainty. "One step at a time. That's all we need."

With a final nod, Caleb slipped out of the church hall, feeling the weight of the evening settle within him. As he stepped into the cool night air, he saw George waiting by the steps, his gaze quiet and determined.

"You heading my way?" George asked, his voice steady.

Caleb asked, "Why didn't you come in?"

"Maryam was too upset seeing me at the last meeting," he answered. "I couldn't do that to her again. I heard everything, though."

"Caleb commented on the meeting. "Feels like there's a long road ahead. But maybe…maybe we're starting on it together."

Together, they walked, two figures against the backdrop of Cedar Valley, their footsteps echoing with a shared purpose that felt as real as the ground beneath them.

📖 A QUIET REFLECTION

In Cedar Valley, belonging was no longer a given; it was something people had to fight for, something fragile yet deeply valued. Maryam's determination to remind her neighbors of their shared humanity echoed through the small acts of kindness she extended. George's cautious hope, Caleb's reluctant steps toward understanding, and Dan's steady resolve all painted a picture of a community at a crossroads.

Belonging wasn't just about being accepted; it was about creating spaces where everyone felt they had a role, a purpose, and a place. Maryam's and Aisha's stories reminded the town that belonging wasn't about erasing differences but embracing them. However hesitant, Caleb's decision to stay involved showed the strength it takes to bridge divides.

Each act of inclusion and empathy strengthened the foundation of a town working to rebuild itself.

As the church hall emptied and the night wrapped Cedar Valley in its quiet stillness, the foundations of something new were being laid. It wasn't perfect, but it was progress. And in a town struggling to redefine itself, progress was everything.

CHAPTER 6
NEIGHBORS IN THE MAKING

As the first light of dawn crept over Cedar Valley, Teresa stood on her front porch, feeling a quiet hum of anticipation that almost masked the anxiety beneath. The chilly morning air carried the scent of crisp winter, a reminder of simpler times when neighbors greeted one another without hesitation. Now, she watched her street with a sharper eye, noticing how some residents avoided even a glance, their steps quick and guarded. Others paused, exchanging cautious smiles that carried more questions than greetings. The weight of the day ahead pressed on her shoulders, but she knew the gathering she had worked on organizing could not wait any longer. Cedar Valley was splintered, and the cracks were too wide to ignore.

Her thoughts turned to her late father, a man who had once been the community's beating heart. He had always told her that the strength of Cedar Valley wasn't in its buildings or traditions—it was in its people, in their willingness to stand together through hard times. Teresa could still hear his voice, steady and calm, reminding her that when division seeped into the town, it wasn't just the community that suffered — it was the soul of the place.

The memory made her stomach tighten. Cedar Valley didn't feel like home anymore. Neighbors who once shared backyard barbecues now passed each other like strangers. The refugees were only part of the equation. The deeper problem, Teresa knew, was the fear that had rooted itself in their hearts. It was fear that made people see enemies where there were none, fear that turned kindness into suspicion. So many refugees were being placed in surrounding towns Cedar Valley residents were becoming more and more concerned about their own fate. They heard the stories of not having enough jobs and community resources for such an influx of people, plus the effects of cultural differences and the rise in crime. Some in town lobbied the mayor to find a loophole, allowing them to avoid accepting anyone in their town, and others reminded the community that they were kind and generous. The conflict turned to distrust of each other's vision for the town's future. Once the townspeople were told so many refugees were arriving that they needed to be housed in the old high school, the division was well on its way to irreparably fracturing their community.

She gripped the porch railing, her knuckles whitening as she steadied herself. Her father had believed in the power of small actions to change the course of a community, and she clung to that belief now. Tonight's meeting wasn't just about the refugees but about giving Cedar Valley a chance to remember who they were before the fear totally took hold.

Taking a deep breath, she readied herself, steeling her resolve. Caleb Mercer appeared on the sidewalk as if on cue, his boots scuffing the pavement with deliberate slowness. His hands were shoved deep into his jacket pockets, his face etched with fatigue and doubt. Caleb looked almost subdued, usually brash and quick-to-anger, but his eyes betrayed a guarded curiosity.

"You ready to start with this?" Caleb's voice carried both resignation and a trace of challenge.

Teresa nodded, holding his gaze. "We have to start somewhere, Caleb. This community can't keep dividing like this. We must find a way to work together again, even if it's hard; we need to embrace these complete strangers."

Caleb shifted his weight, kicking at a pebble on the ground. "Strangers, yeah. But let's be honest — these refugees aren't just strangers. They're different. They don't know Cedar Valley or what this place used to stand for. And they don't care about our problems —they've got their own." He understood both sides; he kept vacillating between fiercely, angrily advocating for them, and then he thought of his and his friends' precarious lives without jobs and essential resources.

Teresa nodded slowly, acknowledging the truth of his words without wavering. "Maybe so. But they came here looking for a fresh start, just like my grandparents did. Just like yours probably did, too. And maybe — just maybe — they could help us find a way back to what we had before all this division."

Caleb looked down, his expression hardening as his boot scraped against the edge of the porch step. "What if they don't want the same Cedar Valley we want? What if all this talk of 'bringing us together' just tears us further apart? We keep focusing so much on their needs; have we even thought of our own people? We never talk about our townspeople having legitimate concerns. It's implied it's all our fault for not helping enough."

"Or" Teresa replied softly, her voice steady with quiet conviction, "maybe they bring something we didn't know we needed — a new perspective, a way to heal in ways we can't see yet. We won't know unless we try."

Caleb exhaled heavily, his frown deepening, yet his eyes softened just a fraction. "All I'm saying is, don't be surprised if people push back. Our people do not feel they are being heard about their needs. Not everyone's as… hopeful as you are. I'll see you at the 10 am meeting."

As Caleb walked off, Teresa watched him go; she was encouraged that he was following through with attending Dan's volunteer meeting. Would he be able to stop his growing doubts? Despite his bad-tempered reputation, she knew he struggled with how to support both the refugees and the Cedar Valley community. The de facto leaders like herself needed to address the thoughts that fed fears rippling just below the surface of Cedar Valley.

Dan observed his small group of volunteers file past the side table, getting their coffee or tea and a plate of Danish and fruit before sitting around the table. They were here to brainstorm how to encourage the town's community to allow the integration of the refugees. He hoped more would show up; some who said they would help must have changed their minds. His faithful few were at the table. His wife, of course, and the teachers, Avery and Teresa, were concerned with children of both groups, wanting them to feel like they belonged and were safe. Maryam demonstrated her Christian love by arranging food for refugee families from both her Deli and local food banks. Dr. Khalid, bringing her seven-year old with her to the meeting, was medically treating refugees at her clinic. Chloe was using her newfound courage to help refugees at the clinic and exploring ways to engage political leaders who should help address concerns and create solutions. Dan was looking forward to hearing what Lars and Caleb had to say – they wrestled with wanting to help both the refugees and townspeople who suffered from similar issues but felt pushed aside and forgotten. To his surprise, Joe, his congregant known for frequently complaining, showed up. He had his familiar tight, determined expression, but his jaw was visibly looser than it had been in weeks. Was he coming around or came to foster dissent?

Dan started the meeting, losing hope that George was coming. He met with him a while back, encouraging him to make efforts to interact with the community purposefully. Accepting George back into the community could be a precursor for townspeople to overcome their resistance to accepting the refugees. Dan was so proud of George when he bravely spoke up at the last meeting. He thought George was overcoming his past.

Rebecca placed paper and pen in front of each attendee.

"We must progress from just talking to taking action so we can move towards healing our town," Dan said. "It's time to write down our ideas and determine actionable steps to implement ideas."

He saw movement at the door from the corner of his eye. George had found a chair and was sitting in the hall, barely visible. Rebecca handed him a pen and paper; since she knew his difficult situation, she did not ask him to join the others at the table. He took no offense. No one else noticed, so Dan did not acknowledge him yet.

"Okay," Dan said, rolling up his sleeves literally and figuratively. "Let's start writing down possible solutions."

The meeting was winding down. George had not said a word, though Dan saw him writing things down. "George," Dan said, "Why don't you join us as we make the final list of our problems and solutions."

George hesitated, looking at his sister for her reaction. She nodded with a small smile. He approached and sat in the nearest chair.

Rebecca was the group's scribe. "We settled on our first action, planning a community fair. The theme will be diverse heritages and unity. We will have booths with cultural food and crafts, artists, games, town history and resources, and the cultural history of our community, including that of the refugees. Attendees are encouraged to dress in their ancestors' cultural attire. Have I covered everything?"

The group nodded their heads.

"That is the fun project. Where the real work is getting the city council and school board involved." Rebecca finished.

Chloe sighed. "I know. I've said I want to be an agent of change in politics, but I do not know where to start."

Teresa spoke up. "Oh, you need to hang out with Avery and me. We'll get you up to speed quickly. We've already approached some political members to join our community meeting tonight."

"I know we've talked about a few other things, but we have enough to do with these two big projects." Dan said, "We will see each other again at tonight's meeting."

Everyone smiled and shook their heads in agreement. They all rose, saying their goodbyes. George moved to leave quickly, but Maryam called after him. "George, we need to talk."

He stopped but did not speak.

Maryam cleared her throat, tears gathering in her eyes. "Can I have a hug?"

He looked up, surprised. Then, he enveloped her in a bear hug while he sobbed along with her. The group of friends nearby felt the forgiveness and love fill the room.

That evening, the community center filled slowly, the air thick with tension and cautious anticipation. The meeting, organized by Teresa and supported by several key voices in the town, had drawn a crowd that was as diverse as it was divided. The recent influx of Afghan refugees had sparked weeks of heated conversations, and tonight, those voices had finally gathered in one room.

George and Maryam sat in the first row, their faces unable to contain their smiles after reconciling after so many years. They were oblivious to the tension around them. After leaving the morning meeting, they spent the afternoon catching up and reminiscing. They giggled and laughed like children over nonsense memories they shared from their childhood. Enjoying the reestablished closeness, neither noticed the rest of their family entering and sitting in the very back. The younger siblings could not help but smile when they saw George and Maryam so happy together. But when they rose to join them, their father only had to put his arm across their mother to return Fatima and Yusuf to their seats. The older brother, Amir, gave them a withering look and crossed his arms. They were there to find out what was happening in their community, not for a family reunion. Their father, Ahmed, would have a serious conversation with Maryam later that night.

Joe sat down near Caleb. "Are we going to get to tell our side of the story at this meeting?" He said sarcastically. "Like the focus is always on the refugees and their needs. Our impoverished residents are forgotten. Who is advocating for them?"

Teresa stood at the front of the meeting room, signaling that the meeting was starting. Her voice was firm and measured as she spoke. "I empathize with the migrants," she began, glancing at the faces around her, "I also know we must acknowledge the pressing issue of equitably sharing resources between the local community and the migrants. This competition is clear, yet the noise in Cedar Valley is amplified by our lack of understanding of these individuals — their culture, religion, and language."

Sitting next to Teresa, Dr. Aisha Khalid raised her hand to speak. Her voice carried the calm authority of a community leader. "We must tackle this issue head-on before misinformation spreads," she said firmly, her words deliberate. "It's a slippery slope when people start blaming migrants for taking their jobs. We've seen it happen before in neighboring cities with tragic results. Let's not let history repeat itself here."

George tentatively raised his hand. "Dr. Khalid, it is true that refugees have taken jobs. At the unemployment office, there is a designated section specifically for them. I've seen it myself."

Suddenly, a man's voice rang out from the back of the room, loud and cutting. "They must leave Cedar Valley! Afghans must go! I've also seen them get hired over us residents!" His words met with a few scattered cheers of agreement, but others shifted uncomfortably in their seats.

Giving the man in the back a dirty look, Caleb said, "The designated area is because they need an interpreter. Of course, the Afghan interpreters who worked with the military know English, but most of their families do not. I have to agree with George though, Dr. Khalid; the unemployment crisis from the plant closure is made even worse with the refugees competing for the few jobs available. Same with other limited community resources. You also said it's only families here at the old high school. No, there are single men I've seen hanging out behind the school, smoking, but do not acknowledge the older men."

"Those are probably their sons; why assume the worst?" Dr. Khalid said.

Caleb thought for a moment, choosing his words carefully. "I've looked some of them in the eye. I recognize that hateful, defiant stare."

Standing at the rear of the hall, Lars Olson spoke up, his voice calm yet filled with conviction. "Most certainly, I tell you," he began, quoting from the New Testament Matthew 25:40, "because you did it to one of the least of these, my brothers, you did it to me." His words hung in the air, quieting the murmurs as many in the audience reflected on their own values. Though not everyone agreed, Lars's statement carried weight, reminding the crowd of the kindness at the heart of their faith.

The man at the back broke the silence, the anger in his voice more restrained, "You can't just care about the refugees. We need to look after our people, too."

Near the front, Avery Sullivan spoke. "Let's not be insensitive," she said, her voice tinged with urgency. "They are scared, just like we are. Somebody must be on their side." She glanced at Chloe Papadakis, who nodded in agreement.

"Yes, we stand together with them and our residents!" Chloe added, her voice clear and resolute. Her words seemed to spark something in the room, perhaps encouraged by the strong young voice, a faint sense of unity emerging amidst the tension.

Dan said, "You are all right. We must help all our brothers and sisters, our residents and new arrivals. Remember when Jesus was asked by a law expert who is my neighbor? Jesus told the parable of The Good Samaritan. Now is a time we are called to be the Good Samaritan."

As Dan's words settled over the crowd, the room remained quiet, tension lingering like an unspoken question. For a moment, no one moved, the weight of his message sinking into the minds of those gathered. Then, from near the back of the hall, an older man with weathered hands and a cautious expression raised his voice.

"I'll admit, I didn't come here tonight planning to change my mind," he began, his voice low but steady enough to carry. "I've been worried— worried about my family, my job, this town. But maybe you're right, Dan. Maybe we've been so caught up in what we're afraid of that we've forgotten what it means to be neighbors."

A few heads turned in his direction, some nodding subtly, others watching him with guarded curiosity.

Lars Olson stepped forward, his calm presence drawing the room's attention again. "Fear is a powerful thing," Lars said, his voice deliberate, measured. "It can divide us if we let it. But it can also remind us of what matters most — our families, faith, and community. If we let fear dictate how we treat one another, we lose sight of who we are. A group of us met this morning, and we think a fun event like a community fair would be an olive branch from both sides to come together, share cultural experiences, and be neighborly."

A young woman with a hesitant smile spoke up from the middle of the room. "I still have my doubts," she admitted, glancing nervously at the faces around her. "But maybe ... maybe this project is a step in the right direction. Maybe it's worth trying."

A soft murmur spread through the crowd, a ripple of tentative agreement. Sitting near the front, Caleb Mercer leaned back in his chair and crossed his arms, his expression thoughtful. "I'll tell you one thing," he said gruffly, breaking the momentary silence. "We're not gonna solve all our problems tonight. But at least we're talkin' about 'em."

This drew a quiet chuckle from a few corners of the room, the tension easing just slightly.

Dan seized the moment, his voice carrying a renewed conviction. "That's all we can do —start somewhere. Small steps, small changes. But together as a community. That's how we find our way forward."

The air in the room felt different. The divisions were still there, sharp and undeniable, but so was something else — a fragile thread of hope that felt real for the first time in a long time.

As the meeting ended, Maryam rose, her voice steady as she offered a prayer. "Dear Father, we have taken up a big task and need your guidance and blessing. Help us on our way and give us the wisdom to foster unity and discernment to navigate challenges. Bless these efforts to restore neighborly love and trust in our town. We ask this in the name of your Son, Yeshua Ha Mashiach. Amen." She looked at George sitting beside her and took his hand as she whispered a prayer of thanks for their reconciliation.

When he sat down, George's hand instinctively slipped into his pocket, finding the menorah in his pocket, rubbing the seven arms of the tiny replica of the Hebrew biblical lampstand his mother gave him on his thirteenth birthday. He rubbed the smooth, worn arms of the lampstand, each ridge a reminder of his mother's stories about their ancestors' perseverance in the face of overwhelming odds. The menorah had always symbolized resilience — a light that refused to be extinguished even in the darkest times.

Tonight, as he felt the weight of the gathering's fragile unity, George held on to the menorah not just as a keepsake but as a promise. It was a reminder that even the smallest light could pierce the shadows of fear and division, offering hope where despair had taken root.

At that moment, surrounded by neighbors still divided but now willing to try, George felt a quiet resolve take root within him. This wasn't just about refugees or locals — it was about rediscovering the strength to believe in something better together. He finally was starting to feel he was home. Not only reconciling with his sister but also feeling reconciled with his Lord. His father's unforgiveness, as a Christian, was a stumbling block that caused George's faith to falter. Being restored to his sister opened him to feel spiritual healing whether his father ever forgave him or not. The Lord forgave him for his crime when he sincerely confessed. He was finally starting to forgive himself.

As the meeting dispersed, the hum of quiet conversations lingered. Small groups formed near the exit, their faces animated with whispered exchanges that carried traces of both hesitation and determination. Some spoke in hushed tones, weighing the risks of stepping forward, while others stood silently, their eyes scanning the room as if searching for reassurance.

Maryam and George lingered by the coffee table; Maryam's hands clasped tightly in front of her as she glanced at Aisha. "Do you think people will really follow through on this?" she asked quietly.

Aisha offered a gentle smile, her voice soft but firm. "It won't happen all at once. But tonight, we saw something shift. Even small steps can lead to something greater."

Nearby, Lars Olson stood with Teresa, Avery, and Chloe, their discussion punctuated by brief nods and thoughtful pauses. Lars adjusted his glasses, his expression pensive. "It's not going to be easy," he admitted. "Old fears don't disappear overnight. But seeing some of these folks willing to listen — it's more than I expected."

Teresa glanced around the room, her gaze lingering on the clusters of neighbors who continued to talk even after the formal meeting had ended. "I think people want this to work," she said, her voice carrying a quiet hope. "Maybe they're tired of the division, of feeling like strangers in their own town."

From across the room, George Khan saw Caleb leaning against the far wall, his arms crossed but his posture less rigid than usual. Their eyes met briefly, and George gave a slight nod. Caleb nodded back before pushing off the wall and heading toward the door. George's optimism continued to grow in his chest.

Standing beside Dan, Rebecca Larson watched as a few people approached to offer their tentative support. One woman, a mother of three, spoke hesitantly. "I don't know if I can do much," she admitted, her voice wavering. "But I'd like to help where I can. Maybe with organizing donations?"

Dan smiled warmly, placing a reassuring hand on her shoulder. "Every bit helps. It's not about how much you do — it's about being part of the effort."

As the room began to empty, the conversations and quiet commitments carried an undercurrent of cautious hope. It wasn't a wave of overwhelming enthusiasm but a slow, deliberate current — a movement that might, with time, carry Cedar Valley toward something better.

More people than expected joined the project, which Teresa proposed and titled **Get to Know the Visitors.** While the primary goal was to build bridges with the refugees, the project also aimed to strengthen the broader Cedar Valley community by addressing local concerns. In addition to providing food, clothing, and blankets, the initiative included specific efforts to connect underserved residents with resources, job opportunities, and community events. By focusing on shared struggles and mutual support, the project reminded everyone that Cedar Valley's strength lay in its ability to care for all its members, new and old. And, of course, planning the Community fair was well on its way to completion.

☐ A QUIET REFLECTION

The evening's meeting was more than a gathering; it was a crossroads for Cedar Valley. Neighbors, once divided by fear and misunderstanding, came together to share their hopes, frustrations, and quiet uncertainties. Caleb's guarded skepticism, George's quiet resolve, and Teresa's determined leadership reflected a town grappling with its identity.

It wasn't perfect—words still carried sharp edges, and fears lingered unspoken. But amidst the tension, small moments of connection began to emerge. Aisha's calm conviction and Maryam's quiet wisdom reminded everyone that strength lies not in uniformity but in understanding. Lars's steady presence and Dan's unyielding faith in the town's healing ability became anchors in an unsteady sea.

For Caleb, the meeting was more than just a chance to observe; it became a test of his willingness to trust and step into the messy rebuilding process. His decision to voice his concerns, even cautiously, hinted at his growing role as both a bridge-builder and a man finding his place in the community.

The Get to Know the Visitors project wasn't just a plan—it was a fragile promise that Cedar Valley could find its way back to what it once was and perhaps even become something greater. Each conversation, gesture, and tentative step forward was a thread in the fabric of a community striving to mend its fractures.

The journey ahead was uncertain, but in that room, for the first time in a long while, there was a shared sense that Cedar Valley might find the courage to believe in something better together.

CHAPTER 7
ASHES AND TRUTH

Maryam, Aisha, and Dan "broke the ice." They approached a couple that Maryam had come to know while delivering food to the old school. Alim had been a university history professor in Afghanistan. Both he and his wife Padam had worked as translators. They had left their modest home and traveled to Pakistan two weeks before the United States pulled out. They were trying to shield their five children from what they knew would be a bloody outcome and to keep their 16-year-old son, Naadir, from being drafted by the Taliban the way his two older siblings had been.

Alim and Padam were quiet, soft-spoken people. Traditionalists, Padam's face beamed with a mix of kind beauty and perpetual sadness from her tan hajib. She wore a light brown jilbab tunic over loose-fitting parting trousers. Alim had adopted cross-cultural attire: a pair of tan pants, a suit jacket, a kurta shirt, and a kufi hat.

The connection had mainly been through Padam and Maryam. Maryam would appear with a grocery wagon packed with freshly baked pastries and a few other items, bringing huge smiles from everyone. It also helped that she was somewhat familiar with the traditions and language. But on this day, she had remained in her deli, busy at work with an order for a wedding. Aisha brought the food that day.

In a meeting room in the old high school administrative office, a small group gathered around a table. Alim, Padam, and their son Naadir were joined by Dan Larson, Avery Sullivan, Caleb Mercer, Lars Olson, and Dr. Aisha Kahlid. Aisha's son Owen also came. He was friends with some boys living at the school, and they were playing behind it. George Khan was running late, which was no surprise to anyone who knew him. Dan spoke for the group.

"It's been difficult," Dan admitted after listening to Alim talk about attempts to assimilate into the community. "People are afraid of what they don't know."

"The same is true with us," Alim acknowledged, his voice low. He rubbed his full dark beard and glanced at his wife before continuing. "Some have ventured outside with mixed results. The doctor and Maryam," he nodded in Aisha's direction, "have been very kind, but then they are familiar with our ways. All we want is to remain at peace and to determine our own futures. Where will we go next? I do not know. However, it is likely that we will not all go together, and some may choose to remain."

"They will need jobs and places to live," Dan said. "They can't stay in the school forever."

Padam smiled and lowered her head.

Alim smiled. "We have discussed that among us. It seems some of our adult members never liked school."

Owen ran back in during the discussions and tugged on his mother's sleeve. His mother hushed him. "Adults are talking," she whispered. Owen tugged again, his face serious, his eyes darting back and forth between his mother and the back door.

"Mom, please come," he whispered urgently.

Realizing something was wrong, Aisha followed Owen outside. Seconds later, they were back.

"Anxiously but with a calm voice, Aisha said, "The children smell smoke. There must be a fire somewhere. And I see smoke out front."

Dan was out of his chair without thinking. He bolted for the front door with Lars close behind and Aisha next. Alim followed. Smoke filled their nostrils and stung their eyes as they opened the door.

Across the street, smoke billowed out the Deli's open window. Flames were visible from the kitchen's flue. "Maryam!" Aisha screamed, her voice cracking as she ran toward the building. Lars caught her arm, pulling her back just as George appeared at a dead run. Caleb tried to grab his arm as he ran by, but George was too fast. He disappeared through the deli's front door into the dense black smoke.

"Get her!" Aisha yelled, struggling against Lars's firm grip. Knowing her best friend was inside brought tears streaming down her face, mixing with the smoke and ash falling gently on all the onlookers.

The fire spread quickly, devouring the back of the building and billowing black smoke from all windows. Firefighters arrived, uncoiling hoses as water gushed forth to battle the blaze.

Dan yelled after them, "Two people are in there!"

"Whereabouts?" They quickly asked.

"Probably the kitchen!" was the panicked answer.

The glance the firemen exchanged drew a sob from Aisha, understanding what it meant.

Moments later, George emerged from the charred building, followed by a fireman. George was coughing and spitting black gunk on the ground, struggling to breathe. He staggered forward, carrying Maryam wrapped in a blackened tablecloth. His grim expression and tears streaking down his face told the story. The fireman helped George lay her gently on the sidewalk. As emergency personnel carefully unwrapped her to check her pulse and start CPR, the onlookers could see significant burns where her devastated body was exposed.

Her hair was nearly singed off. Aisha fell to her knees in grief. There were burns on George's face underneath the soot and tears. He was continually coughing up black soot. Caleb considered removing George from the tragic scene, but he knew it wouldn't work. As the fireman ceased the futile life-saving efforts and moved to cover Maryam's face, George quickly stopped him. He gently cradled his sister against his chest and let out a groaning cry that touched the soul of every onlooker standing there.

Hours later, the fire was finally extinguished, leaving only the charred skeleton of the deli standing.

The whispers began as the news spread of the fire and the loss of Maryam. They were low at first, but they carried sharp edges.

"Was it an accident?"

"Or sabotage?"

"It could be those refugees," someone muttered. "They've been nothing but trouble."

The tension simmering beneath Cedar Valley's surface now boiled over. Accusations flew, targeting the Afghan families who had fled one tragedy only to find themselves blamed for another. New suspicion spread quickly, reigniting fears that had begun dissipating; instead, they resurfaced to deepen the divides further.

Dan stood in the middle of a crowd gathering on Main Street, raising his hands. "Stop this!" he shouted. "We don't know what happened. Blaming people without evidence will only tear us apart. Besides, Maryam was a friend to the refugees, literally feeding them! It makes no sense for anyone to target her!" His plea was met with resistance. Some nodded in agreement, while others turned away, their expressions hard and unforgiving.

Days later, the fire inspector released the results of his investigation. The blaze had started in the kitchen, where a grease fire ignited after Maryam had suffered a fatal heart attack. The truth was both devastating and clarifying. The refugees were innocent. The fire had been a tragic accident, not an act of malice. With deep sorrow, Maryam's obituary was published.

Obituary: Maryam Khan
Published in *Cedar Valley News*
The Cedar Valley community is mourning the loss of Maryam Khan, a beloved figure whose compassion

and dedication to her family and community touched countless lives. Maryam passed away unexpectedly at the age of 48 after suffering a heart attack at Khan's Deli Kitchen, the family business she co-owned with her parents and siblings.

Born to Ahmed and Farah Khan, Maryam was the eldest of seven siblings and a cornerstone of her family. Her deep roots in Cedar Valley reflected her parents' journey from Pakistan, bringing a legacy of faith and hard work that Maryam carried forward. She leaves behind her siblings: Amir Khan, Fatima Azimi, Yusuf Khan, George Khan, Omar Khan, and Layla Karimi. Despite family challenges, Maryam's commitment to unity and love never wavered.

Maryam was the heart of Khan's Deli Kitchen, turning it into a space for delicious food, connection, and community. Her sudden passing has left Cedar Valley in shock, particularly because of the tragic circumstances of her death. As a result of her heart attack, the unattended kitchen lit the Khan's Deli Kitchen on fire, rendering it a total loss. Thanks to the heroic rescue effort by her brother George, Maryam's body was retrieved so her family could lay her to rest.

A devout Christian, Maryam lived her faith through acts of service. She dedicated much of her time to outreach programs, including food drives and community meals, and she played a pivotal role in fostering understanding and unity in Cedar Valley. Her efforts in the *Get to Know the Visitors* project, aimed at bridging divides between residents and newly arrived Afghan refugees, highlighted her commitment to building a better, more compassionate community.

A funeral service will be held at Cedar Valley Community Church this Saturday at 2 PM, with burial to follow at Cedar Valley Memorial Park. The Khan family invites all who knew Maryam to join in celebrating her remarkable life.

"And let us not grow weary in doing good, for in due season we will reap, if we do not give up." Galatians 6:9

At Maryam's memorial service, the town, as well as many Afghan refugees she had come to know, gathered in mourning." Afghans she had come to know. Her father, Ahmad, stood stoically at the front of the church. He spoke with quiet strength weighed down with grief. Caleb stood nearby, interpreting for Maryam's Afghan friends.

"Maryam has done an amazing job with our family's deli since my wife and I retired," he said, his voice steady despite the tears in his eyes. "She loved Cedar Valley; she believed in our townspeople, their ability to rise above fear and hatred. To honor her memory, we must come together in cooperation and compassion. Let tragically losing her be the catalyst to unite us as she wanted."

His words resonated, though the path to healing would not be immediate. Some offered quiet apologies to the Afghan families, their earlier accusations now a source of shame. Others remained distant, their fear not so quickly assuaged. Caleb translated for some Afghans that they also hoped to find common ground, while others were not convinced the divide could be bridged.

Farah sat quietly weeping during the funeral, listening to her husband speak of their daughter's goodness and her belief in forgiveness. They heard about their son's heroic attempt to rescue Maryam. Their shame and pride in George wrestled within them. His actions trying to save a precious life now, whereas a stranger's was taken so long ago. As Ahmad finished his eulogy for his daughter, he looked directly at George. and said, "Thank you for trying to save her."

When Ahmad returned to his seat, he grasped his wife's hand. With a look, they silently agreed it was time. The Savior's way was forgiveness, peace, and generosity—not hatred or shunning. Maryam took the first step of reconciling with George. They needed to take the next step to achieve her goal of mending the rift that had torn their family apart for so long.

When George caught his parents looking back at him, their tearful faces with hesitant smiles filled him with conflicting emotions. Shame and hope warred within him, and unable to bear the weight of their gaze, he darted from the room. Outside, he collapsed onto the steps of the hall, his hands trembling as he buried his face in them, overwhelmed by the pain of old wounds.

A QUIET REFLECTION

The fire, devastating as it was, became a stark reminder of the lingering fears and tensions that had shadowed the community. But it also became a catalyst for change. George's selfless heroism spoke volumes about the strength found in acts of courage, while Dan's unwavering plea for fairness reminded the town of the cost of unfounded fear. As the truth of the fire emerged, it stripped away the veil of suspicion, forcing the community to confront its own biases and fears.

Maryam's legacy became a quiet but powerful call to action. Her life, built on love, service, and faith, challenged Cedar Valley to rise above its divisions. Her loss was a painful one, but it left a lesson that the town could not ignore—that healing and progress required both sacrifice and perseverance.

Though the road to healing remained steep, Maryam's memory urged each person to take the first step—toward forgiveness, understanding, and the belief that even amidst ashes, new growth could emerge.

CHAPTER 8
THE SHIFTING TIDE

George walked to work the morning after Maryam's memorial with a renewed sense of purpose. His steps were light, though he still avoided the main street. He grieved deeply for his sister, tears often filling his eyes. But reconciling with her and sharing a few last prayers with her healed his heart so much that he knew it was a miracle. Forgiving his father for not forgiving him and forgiving himself for his tragic youthful mistakes were all thanks to Maryam's reminder of forgiveness, hers and the Lord's. As he entered the door to his workplace, his phone buzzed. It was his father; they had not spoken since George went to prison over twenty years ago. When his father thanked him directly at Maryam's memorial, George bolted from the room as soon as possible in a panic, not knowing what to think or say; his emotions were raw. This time, he stayed on the line.

"George," Ahmed Khan's voice trembled, a mixture of age and emotion. "Your mother and I... we've been talking. We would like you to come back to the deli. To the family."

George froze, his father's words hitting him like a blast of wind. He couldn't remember the last time his father had spoken to him without disdain. Slowly, he whispered, "Are you sure?"

"We're sure. Are you ready?" Ahmed asked, his tone resolute. "Maryam would have wanted this."

"Yes, she would. She told me so when we reunited." George could say no more; he choked up, remembering her sincere prayer for a family reunion.

"Come to dinner tonight; we must get reacquainted. It will make your mother very happy."

The call ended, leaving George in stunned silence. His parents had reached out for the first time in years—not with judgment, but with an olive branch.

George's actions during the fire and the inspector's findings continued to spread within the refugee community. Alim and Padam, respecting George's bravery, gave him a small gift. Maryam had become a close friend of theirs, giving to him eased their grief from losing her. George accepted it humbly, giving all the glory to God. This act of gratitude from a refugee family softened many hearts in Cedar Valley. While not everyone was ready to embrace the "visitors," the gesture shifted the tone of the town's conversations. Neutrality, if not acceptance, began to take hold in the hearts of some of the community's strongest skeptics.

Dan Larson sat near the front of the town hall; his usually calm demeanor betrayed by the tension in his furrowed brow. On the surface, the community meeting was progressing as planned. Teresa Nikas spoke with her characteristic poise, Caleb Mercer raised valid, if skeptical, questions, and Chloe Papadakis shared her optimistic vision for refugee integration. Yet, Dan felt as though he was striding through a cloud of swirling, hot ash from a fire whose origin he could not determine.

Dan felt crushed, not by one incident but by the accumulation of tensions that were still trying to choke the life out of Cedar Valley. Maryam's and Dr Khalid's efforts moved the townspeople and refugees towards unifying into one community. Recent events threatened the momentary neutrality when Maryam tragically died. Without her de facto leadership of steady, faithful compassion, there was no clear path forward, no distinguishable horizon for the promised resolution. This was his community, currently a battlefield for peace and harmony, and they had no alternative homeland for escape. As the bishop of this ward, Dan knew he had to keep leading the community forward to peaceful coexistence, even though right now, he felt blind and ineffective.

Chloe's voice rose, cutting through the dense fog of Dan's thoughts. "Legislation provides comprehensive protections for the rights of refugees, enabling access to employment, education, healthcare, housing, social security benefits, and family reunification opportunities akin to those afforded to citizens.

Dan hoped her optimism was infectious. However, he wondered how many in the room believed her words could bridge the divide.

Caleb Mercer, his arms crossed, his skepticism visible in his furrowed brow. "Are you suggesting these individuals will integrate seamlessly into our systems? When our own people don't feel the system works for them?" he asked, his tone challenging but not dismissive.

"Certainly," Chloe affirmed, her confidence unwavering. "Their integration can positively influence both societal and economic structures."

"How?" Caleb responded. "I think you are naïve; your youthful exuberance hasn't yet faced life's hard lessons. Economically? You need to demonstrate actionable steps towards economic progress, like we are planning social events which aim to integrate our communities into one. When I say demonstrable economic steps, none have been offered that I know of."

The room shifted slightly as heads nodded cautiously, agreeing that having social events was promising. It wasn't outright agreement, but it was a start. However, the economic protections afforded refugees were a sore subject for many. The townspeople struggled with endless government red tape to get assistance, but the refugees seemed to get their aid without the same efforts.

Dan looked at the faces around him—some skeptical, others hopeful, many simply weary. The community was fractured, but it was not beyond repair. He knew the solution wasn't about defeating the opposition but showing the skeptics on both sides how they could live in harmony with each other when both groups have their fears allayed.

Cedar Valley was a microcosm of America, a nation built by people who didn't always agree but still managed to construct a foundation that was the world's envy.

When George Khan stood to speak, Dan felt a pang of uncertainty. Though he encouraged George to speak up and proactively re-enter society, how negative would he be after the death of his sister and since he was directly affected by the economic crisis?

"Understanding and empathy can bridge divides," George said, his voice steady but tinged with the weight of his past. "We need to show that we are willing to listen and learn, as do the refugees. Maryam began work on that bridge; we all must finish building it. That's the only way forward."

His words resonated. Even Caleb nodded slightly, his skepticism momentarily tempered by the truth in George's statement.

Teresa retook the rostrum, her voice filled with quiet determination. "This community has faced challenges before, and we've risen above them—not because it was easy, but because it was necessary and the right thing to do. We can do it again." Her gaze swept the room, meeting Dan's briefly, and he felt a flicker of hope. "The last meeting Maryam was at we talked about a Community Fair. She loved the idea. We need to proceed with it with as much enthusiasm as she had. And we will name it Maryam's Community Fair."

"Is it the right time for such a thing?" someone asked. "The family is still grieving."

"I am sure her family will welcome honoring her." Dan stood to address the room for the meeting's closing words. "We've got work to do," he said. "This isn't easy, and not everyone will agree. But we owe it to each other—to ourselves and the refugees—to try." Impulsively, Dan added, "For those who want to, please stay with me to pray for the unity of our town."

Many people joined him, relaxing the tension in his body, giving his faith space to remind him he always had access to hope. Finishing the prayer, Dan felt a measure of clarity. The road ahead was uncertain, but he was no longer walking blind. This was his community, and he would fight to save it—not with frustration but with hope, determination, and understanding.

Grief is a wound that becomes infected the more you scratch it. The only recourse is to let the scar thicken, but even that doesn't make it disappear. It never truly heals. It rests in the bones, settling into the marrow like embers that unexpectedly burst into raging fires and then quiet again.

Aisha Khalid lay in bed, muffling her cries into a pillow. The weight of loss—Maryam's death and the simmering tensions in Cedar Valley—pressed down on her chest. She wanted to be strong for her son, Owen, but strength felt like a fleeting shadow beyond her grasp.

Morning prayers, once a source of stability, now felt like a burden too heavy to bear. She closed her eyes, willing herself to rise but finding no energy.

A soft knock interrupted her thoughts, and she opened the door to find Owen standing there with his prayer rug in hand. His face was earnest, his eyes heavy with concern.

"I want to pray Fajr with you, Mama," he said softly.

Aisha looked down at him fondly, brushing her tears away. "You brought your rug," she noted with a faint smile.

The small rug in his hands was brightly colored, adorned with golden arches and green vines. It had been a birthday gift, given to him when he turned six—a way to gently introduce him to the practice of prayer and the tradition of faith that anchored their family. He had treasured it ever since, spreading it out beside hers each time he joined her in prayer.

"You're such a good boy, Owen," she said, her voice catching. "Let's go."

They entered the living room together, where Aisha spread her prayer rug, its intricate geometric patterns facing the qibla, the direction of Mecca. Owen followed her lead, carefully unrolling his rug beside hers. Though different in size and design, the rugs symbolized the same thing: a sacred space, free from distractions, dedicated to connecting with God.

As they began their prayers, their voices blended in quiet harmony. Aisha recited the verses of the Quran with practiced fluency, her words steady despite the heaviness in her heart. Owen followed as best as he could, his small voice joining hers during the phrases he remembered.

The prayer shared between mother and son brought a sense of calm that had eluded her all morning.

Outside, on Aisha's front porch, George sat holding a hot cup of coffee in both hands, staring into the distant dawn on the horizon. He found Aisha's home calm, rich with the aroma of spices, and warm with conversations based on their common love for his sister. He could barely hear the quiet murmur of Aisha and Owen praying, finding the sound soothing. Maryam often brought breakfast for the pair before she opened the deli. George followed the tradition when he could. The timing often coincided with their morning prayers since baking at the Deli started well before dawn. Thankfully, while the decision of how the Deli would be rebuilt, the city allowed the Khans to use the old high school's kitchen so they could stay in business. Following Maryam's breakfast habit reminded him of his last conversation with her when she said faith is a bridge, not a wall. Inspired by the memory, he brought his Bible to share today.

When the prayers ended, Aisha turned to Owen and tightly hugged him. "You did well, my son," she said, her voice filled with pride.

George knocked on the door and stepped in when she opened it. Handing her the bag of breakfast food, he gently asked, "May I join you?"

Aisha nodded, a flicker of warmth breaking through her grief. "Of course."

He held his Bible up, saying, "Maryam reminded me of the importance of prayer and Bible study, something I wish I hadn't forgotten. I'd like to pray with you. Is that okay?"

"Certainly." She said, Owen looking on curiously.

George sat on the couch, opened his Bible, and read Psalm 23. Soon, he would again be able to say it from memory. Then he began to pray aloud, his words heartfelt and straightforward. He gave thanks for the city's generosity to keep their business open and asked for guidance and healing for the days ahead. Aisha and Owen listened silently; George's voice momentarily lifted their shared grief. Though their prayers differed, the room was filled with a profound sense of peace, a sanctuary created by their shared humanity.

The quiet of the morning gave way to the slow rhythms of the day. George returned to his parents' home, where visitors were still coming by, offering food, condolences, and stories of Maryam. Though marked by sorrow, the house became a place of connection for the whole community. Refugee families and longtime residents shared tea and conversation, bridging divides in ways that might have seemed impossible weeks ago. Small acts of kindness rippled outward, softening the sharp edges of grief and prejudice. For the first time in a long while, the future didn't feel as bleak.

Beyond the house, beyond the front gate, beyond the sidewalk that wove around the adjacent blocks, a ripple of understanding spread through the neighborhood. Alim and Padam reminded Dan of the community fair idea Maryam told them about at the meeting where she and George reconciled. Teresa and Avery began planning in earnest to ensure the project blossomed into a successful town fair.

"I'd like to join you in planning the fair, as I am sure Maryam would have. Grieving her loss will never stop," Padam told Teresa and Avery as she thought of her two sons she lost to the Taliban. "We can only treat the wounds to heal as much as possible. Working on community unity with you will be healing for my family and others. Maryam sincerely wanted this to happen."

As it was called, Maryam's Community Fair would be an event of shared cultures. The townspeople and immigrant newcomers would bring their best ideas together. There would be booths of food, traditional arts, craftworks, clothing, and music. Like Avery's idea of having the school children explore their family histories, the event would highlight individuals and groups' unique and similar characteristics. The children wanted a booth to display their projects. Chloe would have a booth educating about the history and rules of voting. Since she registered, she completed intense research for accurate information. For example, she learned that voter registrars cannot advise people how to vote. Only the resources available to determine for themselves. They also had to verify if a person was legally allowed to register.

Maryam, the woman who had been a fragile thread between the two camps as she shuttled back and forth with her baked goods, was now, in death, a healing salve for the community. The quiet echo of her generosity and compassion lived on in the growing bridge. Some still grumbled and complained that it wouldn't work to bring people together. But people's fondness for Maryam in both communities stifled those doubts and hopes grew for the friendships that would emerge from the gathering. Many were determined to move towards one united community, creating a jointly successful future for Cedar Valley.

The Maryam Community Fair was a resounding success. For readers of *Cedar Valley News*, reading of the joyful event was cathartic and lessened fears.

> ### *Cedar Valley News*:
> **United at the multicultural Maryam Community Fair**
> *By Sarah Whitman, Staff Reporter*
> The sound of laughter, music, and the scent of home-cooked meals filled the air this past weekend as Cedar Valley came together for the much-anticipated multicultural Community Fair. Held in the town square, the event was a beacon of hope and unity in a community facing significant challenges recently.
> The Community Fair, organized to celebrate Cedar Valley's rich diversity and shared heritage, was a resounding success. What began as a simple idea to foster understanding between longtime residents and the town's Afghan refugee newcomers quickly became a day of joy, reflection, and connection. It was named in celebration of our dear Maryam Khan, remembered for her self-sacrifice and compassion for residents and refugees alike.
> From morning to evening, the square buzzed with activity. Booths displayed traditional crafts, foods, and clothing from various cultural backgrounds, while local artists and performers lent their talents to a small but vibrant stage. One of the event organizers, Teresa Nikas, said, "This fair wasn't just about celebrating

our differences—it was about discovering the shared threads that bind us all together as a community."

One unforgettable highlight came when Lars Olsen, known for his typically calm, business-like demeanor, became swept up in the day's spirit. Dressed in his family's tartan, Lars brought his grandfather's bagpipe to life. The mournful yet hopeful notes echoed across the park, drawing smiles and applause from the crowd. Children twirled and danced in the grass, their laughter rising with the music, while others watched from porches and picnic blankets.

Sitting with her son Owen and George Khan on her front porch, Aisha Khalid reflected on the moment. "Hearing the bagpipes and seeing the children's joy— these are moments when you feel the weight lift, even if just for a little while," Aisha said with a faint but warm smile.

The fair wasn't only about entertainment. It also served as an opportunity for education and bridge-building. Avery Sullivan and her students presented their history project tracing the ancestry of Cedar Valley's residents, creating a powerful reminder that many of the town's families were once newcomers themselves. Some families had ancestors who were always from the local area, indigenous, or of origin lost to history. "Seeing the origins of our neighbors' stories gave me hope that this town can embrace new ones," Avery shared.

The day also included booths sharing dishes from long-time residents and refugee families. The spicy aroma of Afghan kebabs mingled with the rich, buttery scent of traditional Southern biscuits—a culinary metaphor for the cultural blending the Village Fair hoped to achieve. Another event organizer, Dan Larson, took a moment to address the crowd. "Today, we proved that Cedar

Valley is more than its divisions. We're a community. We're neighbors. And together, we can build a bridge to something stronger."

The Maryam Community Fair ended with lanterns being released into the sky, a symbolic gesture of shared hopes for a brighter, more united future and in memory of the light of friendship Maryam was the first to inspire. For a town with so many uncertainties, the fair was a testament to what can be achieved when people come together with open hearts and minds.

As residents returned home, the echoes of bagpipes, laughter, and shared stories lingered. Cedar Valley had a long way to go in healing its divisions, but the community fair was a hopeful, beautiful step in the right direction.

A QUIET REFLECTION

Cedar Valley was slowly but surely learning that healing could come in unexpected ways. The Maryam Community Fair, born from shared grief and cautious hope, became more than an event—a turning point. The children's laughter, shared stories, and the melodies of bagpipes weaving through the air were proof that connection could outshine division.

Maryam's memory had become a thread of unity, her kindness and resilience inspiring both longtime residents and newcomers. The fair, with its vibrant booths and cultural exchange, was a testament to what Cedar Valley could be—a community not defined by its fractures but by its efforts to bridge them.

In that moment, as lanterns rose into the night sky, their soft glow casting warmth over the gathering there was a shared understanding: progress was possible. Though it was clear that the town's journey was far from over, they were finding a way forward. Through music, food, and conversation, Cedar Valley had taken a step toward something brighter—a community built not on fear but on the quiet strength of coming together.

CHAPTER 9
NEIGHBORS OR STRANGERS

A quiet, joyful peace had settled over the Khan household, though the ache of Maryam's loss lingered. Her absence was deeply felt in the daily rhythms of their lives, from the laughter she brought to her quiet wisdom. Her legacy of kindness and resilience had left an indelible mark. As Christians, the family found solace in the belief that Maryam was safe in the arms of their Savior. They clung to the hope that one day, they would meet again in glory.

George sat with his father in the living room after supper. The warm glow of a table lamp illuminated the room, its gentle light falling on family photos lining the walls. The air between them was cautious but warm, the years of estrangement giving way to the first tentative steps of reconciliation.

"You know, George," his father began, his voice tinged with emotion, "it is such a relief that things seem to be settling down in our city. And, son, most of all, I am so happy you are back with us. You'll never know how much we missed you. I am truly sorry for everything that happened and how we reacted."

George met his father's eyes, the sincerity in his voice melting the years of bitterness that had built up like an unscalable wall. "Dad, it's okay. I brought it upon myself with my poor choices and the friends I had then. I brought shame upon our family. I never stopped loving you, praying I'd be forgiven and see my family again. Now, we have forgiven each other! From here, we will be looking forward."

His father smiled, a rare, vulnerable moment that reminded George of his childhood. "Fine with me. It all seems part of what is happening in the town as well. People seem to be moving back toward unity and empathy."

George nodded thoughtfully. "True, and soon, those scoundrels behind all this strife and division will be exposed. I hope they will get what they deserve."

"They surely will," his father said, tapping the newspaper with troubling articles about crime and those forcing dissension. "Justice always prevails. Soon, there will be peace here and throughout the country again."

"That I'm not so sure of," George replied, leaning back into the couch. "It is, after all, a two-way street. Not all the rumors of immigrant trouble are untrue. In some other towns, unsavory elements did seep in to disrupt, with the purpose of taking over."

His father raised an eyebrow, his tone skeptical but open. "What makes you so sure?"

"When I was inside, a few inmates talked about it," George said quietly, his words hanging in the air.

"And you believe inmates?"

George chuckled softly. "I was one of them, remember? You get to know who talks trash and who is sincere. Some of them told horrible stories of immigrants wrecking town centers if they didn't get their way. Of course, we don't think those guys were truly refugees. They just posed as refugees to infiltrate communities and take control. One inmate told how he defended his family during a riot, knocking down one of them. But who got arrested? He did, not the guy who was rioting and breaking shop windows."

His father sighed, rubbing his hands together slowly. "Well, we are blessed to have true refugees, many of whom are Christian brothers and sisters."

"Absolutely. Father is merciful to have spared our town such troubles. Perhaps incidents like that, however, isolated, flamed the idea behind the flood of misinformation to spread nationwide fear and hatred for all immigrants."

"That is quite possible," his father agreed. "Anyhow, I am very happy things are turning around in our city. It will take time and work, but I believe in the end, everything will get back to where we were, and even better, having made new friends and harvesting the benefits of the skills and positive contributions of those who have come to us for refuge and help."

"Absolutely." Changing the subject, George said, "Did you know Maryam often brought Aisha and Owen breakfast before opening the Deli? I'm continuing her practice. I often arrive early enough to sit on her porch and listen to her and Owen pray. It's soothing. So, I recently brought my Bible and prayed with them.

His father's head snapped up, his face etched with surprise. "You did what?"

"I prayed with Aisha," George said.

"Now, son," his father said, leaning forward, "you know you cannot do that."

"Why not? Because she is Muslim?"

"Yes, exactly. You know the difference between us and Islam. You cannot mix the two."

George frowned, his tone turning reflective. "Isn't that part of the division among all the townspeople?"

His father shook his head, his voice softening. "Not exactly. It is one thing to work together in peace, understanding, and acceptance of individuals, but to mix two very different religions and try to make them one cannot work. It's like marriage. Your mother has her personality, I have mine, and we live together in harmony, not because we have become like each other, but because we have learned to bypass differences with love and loyalty."

George nodded slowly, letting the words settle. "You mean I can support Aisha and Owen in all matters but not worship with them?"

"Exactly. She is lovely, and we'll never turn our backs on her. Keeping us from worshiping with her does not mean we are divided. Just different."

George sighed, his father's words stirring a deep conflict within him. "Okay. I get your point, and I'll think about it. I'll also inquire of the Spirit of God for confirmation."

"You do that, son. Do that," his father said, resting a hand on George's shoulder.

More and more concerning articles were published about the burgeoning community conflicts stoked by subversive efforts. These many exaggerations and outright lies anonymously spread among the townspeople and kept the fear alive.

Cedar Valley News
Unmasking the Forces Dividing Our Community
By Sarah Whitman, Staff Reporter

Once a beacon of unity and understanding, Cedar Valley has recently become the center of misinformation and division. Recent events suggest that more than the arrival of migrant families is at play. Evidence points to organized efforts—local and external—leveraging misinformation to pit neighbors against neighbors, dismantling the compassion that has long defined our community.

The Arrival of Migrants: Compassion Meets Controversy

For decades, Cedar Valley has prided itself on being a welcoming town rooted in Christian values of charity and kindness. The town is now facing an unprecedented economic downturn, accompanying shortages, and other related burdens. The recent arrival of migrant families fleeing violence and seeking better lives has further challenged the good townspeople to maintain their generous and caring character towards strangers who are from a war-torn country and a significantly different culture.

Mobilized by an ad-hoc group of community leaders, churches and individuals joined together to provide food and clothing for the refugees housed by the town in the old high school. However, as weeks pass, fear and division continue to sweep through the town, fueled by rumors and accusations. Community leaders began to notice patterns in these tensions. Narratives emerged that were eerily similar to those seen in other communities grappling with migration. it was determined these narratives weren't organically born but appeared orchestrated to unravel Cedar Valley's social fabric.

Cedar Valley News
Misinformation Sources Targeting Cedar Valley
By Sarah Whitman, Staff Reporter
Cedar Valley's experience echoes incidents across the country where misinformation, based on partial truths, amplified strategically and deployed to sow discord. Following are examples:

1. **Fake Social Media Accounts**: Anonymous accounts have flooded local Facebook groups with exaggerated and outright false claims, such as allegations of migrant families committing crimes or consuming public resources disproportionately. These posts often lack evidence but generate heated arguments among residents.

2. **Fabricated Stories of Migrant Misconduct**: Similar to the debunked narrative in Ohio of Haitian migrants consuming pets (though the gang problems have some truth to them), Cedar Valley has faced baseless fantastical rumors. One persistent claim involves unfounded allegations of vandalism attributed to migrant youth despite no reports from local law enforcement.

3. **Inflammatory Terms Like 'Invasion'**: Some outside commentators have described the migration as an "invasion," language previously debunked in national contexts but now weaponized to polarize Cedar Valley's residents. This rhetoric distorts the reality that most migrants are families seeking safety and opportunity.

4. **False Claims About Government Benefits**: Emails and posts circulating falsely allege that migrants receive extensive government checks, sparking resentment among locals. Officials confirm these claims are invalid; migrants in Cedar Valley receive support primarily through nonprofit organizations and local charity efforts.

5. **Anonymous Flyers and Leaflets**: Flyers found around town claim that the migrant families are members of criminal gangs. Law enforcement has thoroughly investigated and dismissed these claims as unfounded, but the damage to trust within the community lingers.

6. **Weaponizing Religious Values**: Some misinformation campaigns have targeted Cedar Valley's faith-based organizations, accusing them of prioritizing migrants over long-time residents. This narrative aims to fracture the collaboration between churches and civic groups.

Cedar Valley News
The Evidence of Organized Forces
By Sarah Whitman, Staff Reporter
Cedar Valley News has uncovered links between some of these misinformation efforts and national groups known for exploiting migration issues to promote division. Analysts point to a deliberate strategy:

- **Social Media Amplification**: Troll farms and bots have been identified as spreading anti-migrant content in local forums.

- **Coordinated Narratives**: Messaging aligns closely with themes seen in other towns, suggesting centralized coordination.
- **Exploitation of Local Tensions**: Outside forces use real, localized challenges—like resource constraints—to magnify fear and mistrust.

These campaigns aim to dismantle Cedar Valley's historic unity by framing migration as a zero-sum issue, where one group's gain must come at another's loss.

Fighting Back: A Unified Response

Despite these challenges, Cedar Valley has seen glimmers of hope. Leaders from various faiths, local officials, and grassroots organizers are working together to counteract misinformation. Community meetings have been held to share accurate information and foster dialogue.

Law enforcement and independent researchers actively monitor misinformation sources, ensuring Cedar Valley residents have access to facts. Churches have redoubled their efforts to bridge divides, offering workshops on cultural understanding and the importance of unity.

Moving Forward as One Community

Cedar Valley's challenges are not unique but emblematic of broader struggles in a disinformation age. What sets this town apart is its commitment to overcoming division through empathy and action. As one local pastor remarked, "We are a town of neighbors, not strangers. If fear dictates our actions, we lose who we are."

Cedar Valley News hopes to empower residents to reject fear and falsehoods by illuminating these organized efforts to divide. Together, Cedar Valley can reaffirm its identity as a compassionate, unified community, resilient against those who seek to undermine its values.

Letter to the Editor

Dear Editor,

These are not migrants, who primarily move looking for work; these are refugees, who must flee their country to avoid persecution, violence and even death. Many of these individuals risked their lives to help America when it was in Afghanistan. They immigrated because, if they had stayed, the Taliban would have killed them. These are not the disreputable or undesirables of their country. Many are professionals—doctors, merchants, and skilled workers—who are now seeking safety and a chance to rebuild their lives here in Cedar Valley.

We must ask ourselves this: Will we provide refuge as our values demand, or will we spread hatred and fear? Our country was founded on principles of freedom, liberty, and the pursuit of happiness. These principles were hard-won by our forefathers, who believed every individual deserved a chance to thrive. Now, we stand at a crossroads. Will we honor these principles or let fear and prejudice dictate our actions? It is our choice.

For those who wish to assist—whether through food, clothing, language classes, or employment opportunities—or those who want to meet our new neighbors, we invite you to join us. We meet in the lunchroom of the old high school at 9 a.m., Monday through Thursday.

Let us be the community we claim to be—compassionate, united, and strong in the face of fear.

Sincerely,

Chloe Papadakis

Concerned Citizen of Cedar Valley

Cedar Valley had always prided itself on being a community of shared values—a place where neighbors greeted each other by name and doors were left unlocked without a second thought. Yet the arrival of Afghan refugees had tested the boundaries of that identity, forcing the town to confront the newcomers and its hidden fractures.

Misinformation and fear had seeped into the cracks of Cedar Valley's unity, sowing division among its residents. But there was also a spark of hope for every whisper of distrust. People like Teresa Nikas, Dan Larson, and Aisha Khalid had begun organizing gatherings and conversations, determined to remind Cedar Valley of the compassion that once defined it.

THE CHURCH BASEMENT MEETING: A FRACTURED COMMUNITY CONVENES

The basement of First Presbyterian Church was packed with more than thirty residents, the air heavy with anticipation. Teresa stood at the front, her posture confident, though her heart raced like a caged bird. She had spent nights rehearsing her opening words, questioning whether she was the right person to mend a community so frayed. Still, there was no turning back.

Behind her, a projector displayed a stark headline: Refugees Overrun Local Resources—Tensions Rise in Small Towns.

"These headlines are designed to divide us," Teresa began, her voice steady despite her nerves. "to make us afraid of each other. And they're working. However, though local resources are stretched further than ever, many in the community have come together and are resolving the problems with creative solutions. Therefore, all needs are being met."

She clicked to the next slide, which showed inflammatory social media posts accusing refugee families of everything from vandalism to draining welfare systems. The images ignited a low murmur among the crowd. She could feel Caleb Mercer's gaze boring into her from the back wall. He crossed his arms, his posture bristling with skepticism.

"And how do you know it's not true?" Caleb asked, his tone cutting. "What if these people are trouble? What if they're not here to join us but to take over?"

Teresa inhaled deeply. "Because we've done the research, Caleb. Law enforcement has found no evidence of these claims in Cedar Valley, though it's true that other towns in the county have to deal with increased crime. But those fearful in our town don't need facts— just a story."

A resident, seated in the front row, scoffed audibly. His voice carried through the tense silence as he spoke. "You keep saying it's lies, but what about the truth? I've seen the stats. You're right; the problems are primarily in other towns. Ours has a minor uptick, and it's ignored. Besides, these people don't share our values. They don't speak our language. They don't belong here."

Sitting near the front, Aisha Khalid felt the familiar weight of such comments pressing down on her chest. She had heard them before—in airports, supermarkets, and whispers. Straightening her shoulders, she chose her moment carefully.

"These families aren't here to take from us," Aisha said, her voice calm but resolute. "They're here to escape violence, to rebuild their lives. But if we shut them out, we're turning our backs on the very values this town claims to stand for."

Across the room, Chloe Papadakis raised her hand. Her tone was measured but tentative. "I get where the man is coming from," she said. "Change is hard. But isn't that why we're here? To figure out how to move forward together instead of letting this tear us apart?"

Dan Larson stood, his voice carrying the weight of years spent mediating disputes. "Look," he said, "we've been here before—every wave of immigrants—whether they were Irish, Italian, or Mexican—faced suspicion. But over time, they became part of the community. That's what's going to happen here if we let it."

The room fell quiet, Dan's words settling over the crowd like a balm. Teresa scanned the faces in the room, searching for signs of progress. Even Caleb, though still guarded, seemed to be listening more closely than before.

As the meeting dispersed, Teresa lingered near the podium, exhaustion settling into her bones. Aisha approached her with a soft smile.

"You did well," Aisha said. "It's not easy standing up to all of that."

Teresa nodded, her gratitude evident. "I couldn't have done it without you."

CALEB'S REFLECTION

Caleb sat on the worn bench outside his house, the faint smell of pine lingering in the cool night air. He ran his fingers over the armrest, the wood polished smooth by years of use. His family had lived in Cedar Valley for generations, their roots intertwined with the town's history. Yet, for all his talk of belonging, Caleb couldn't shake the nagging voice in the back of his mind.

His great-great-grandfather arrived in Cedar Valley with nothing but a toolbox and a stubborn determination to make a life. The townspeople were initially wary, suspicious of his thick accent and strange customs. But over time, he had won them over and became a fixture in the community. Caleb had heard the stories countless times, but tonight, they felt more significant.

"What would he think of me now?" Caleb muttered to himself. He thought of the church meeting, of George's, other resident's sharp words, and Aisha's quiet defiance. He didn't want to admit it, but something about Aisha's story had struck a chord. Maybe it was how her voice trembled slightly when she spoke of rebuilding lives. Or maybe the realization that his family's story wasn't so different from hers just started in an earlier century.

AT LARS OLSON'S HARDWARE STORE: PLANS TAKE SHAPE

"We need more actions, "Lars said, his steady voice anchoring the discussion. . More community events, shared meals, events to remind people that we're all in this together. The Fair was such a success, you could see and feel the connections forming."

Rebecca Larson, her hands clasped tightly in her lap, spoke up. "The Bible says, 'You shall not wrong a stranger or oppress him, for you were strangers in the land of Egypt.' That's what we're forgetting. That's what we're called to remember."

George, who had joined after the church meeting, nodded slowly. He glanced at Lars before speaking. "Fear doesn't come from what we know, its from what we don't understand. We need to ask more questions, share more about ourselves and our town with the newcomers."

Caleb, who had been silent up to this point, leaned forward. His brow furrowed in thought. "It's not just about being neighbors—it's about accountability," he said. "We've let these partial truths and lies take root because it was easier than confronting the truth. But if we want things to improve, we must do better."

The group nodded in agreement, their murmurs carrying a newfound sense of purpose. Rebecca looked around the room, her heart swelling with cautious hope. "Then let's do it," she said. "Let's remind this town who we are. Let's host a multicultural meal to show our hospitality."

A SHARED MEAL AT THE COMMUNITY CENTER

The community center buzzed with activity as residents and newcomers gathered for a potluck dinner. Afghan families brought dishes rich with spices and flavors, while longtime Cedar Valley residents contributed casseroles, pies, and sweet tea. The scent of cumin and cinnamon mingled with the aroma of baked apples and fried chicken, filling the air with a sense of cautious harmony.

Aisha watched as Owen, her son, sat beside an Afghan boy his age, the two laughing and sharing stories despite the language barrier. Their hands darted toward the same dish, a plate of fried pakoras, and they dissolved into giggles. The sight warmed her heart, a reminder of how children often found ways to connect where adults struggled.

Nearby, Ruth, a long-time resident known for her sharp tongue, stood at the refreshment table, staring down a biryani dish with narrowed eyes. Aisha hesitated before stepping forward.

"Would you like to try some?" Aisha asked gently, holding out a small plate.

Ruth's lips pursed as she accepted the plate. "I don't know if I'll like it," she said, her tone teetering between skepticism and curiosity.

Aisha smiled. "That's all right. If you don't, I can recommend the casserole—it's my favorite."

Ruth took a small bite. Her expression softened as the flavors settled on her tongue. "It's... different," she said. Then, almost reluctantly, she added, "But not bad."

The moment felt small, but it carried its own weight—it was a quiet bridge between two worlds.

Across the room, Caleb found himself standing beside George. He seemed lost in thought, his gaze sweeping over the room as he watched residents and newcomers share food and tentative smiles.

"They're not so different, are they?" Caleb said quietly, surprising even himself.

George's lips twitched, though it wasn't quite a smile. "Maybe not. But it will take more than a few meals to fix this."

"Yeah," Caleb agreed. "But it's another step towards unity."

Teresa sat with Rebecca Larson at a nearby table, who had just returned from leading the evening's prayer. Rebecca leaned in, her voice soft but firm.

"You're doing good work here, Teresa," Rebecca said. "But don't forget to take care of yourself. Even shepherds need rest."

Teresa smiled, though it didn't quite reach her eyes. "I'll rest when the work is done."

ECHOES OF THE COMMUNITY FAIR

The sense of unity in the room felt fragile, like a thread stretched thin, but it was there, nonetheless.

Lars found himself thinking about the Community Fair from a few weeks ago. Up to that point, he had been skeptical about the likelihood of bringing the community together. But the atmosphere was in harmony. He'd surprised even himself by donning his family's tartan and playing his grandfather's bagpipes. The haunting melody had drawn children into an impromptu dance, their laughter echoing across the fairgrounds.

He hadn't planned to play. It was supposed to be a quiet evening—just him and the familiar comfort of watching from the sidelines. But something stirred in him as he watched the Afghan and Cedar Valley children running and laughing together. Before he knew it, the pipes were in his hands; he brought it to the event for display as an ancestral heirloom, and the music was in the air.

The memory brought warmth to his chest, even now. Maybe, just maybe, there was hope for this town after all.

HOPE FOR TOMORROW

As the evening wound down, Teresa stepped to the front of the room. She was tired—bone-tired—but the sight of the community gathered together gave her the strength to speak one more time.

"This has been a hard road," she began, her voice steady despite the weariness etched in her features. "Tonight, I see connection growing. We need to keep talking, listening, and gathering so we can rebuild what fear tried to take from us."

The room filled with applause—not the raucous cheers of a crowd but the quiet clapping of people who understood the work ahead and were willing to try. The hum of conversation began to fade, replaced by the soft clinking of plates being gathered and chairs being stacked.

Outside, Caleb and George walked together under the fading light of the day, their steps slow and deliberate. The air was crisp, with the faint scent of autumn leaves and distant chimneys.

"You think this'll work?" Caleb asked, his tone skeptical but not unkind.

George considered the question for a moment. "I think it has to. We don't have another option."

Caleb nodded slowly, his hands shoved deep into his coat pockets. "Yeah. I guess you're right."

They walked silently for a while, their footsteps blending with the rustle of leaves and crunch of snow. As they reached the edge of the park, George paused, turning to look back at the community center. The warm glow of lights spilled out into the darkness, accompanied by the faint hum of laughter and conversation. He knew Maryam would have been in there, faithfully cleaning up and restoring order, chatting and laughing with everyone.

"It's not perfect," George said. "But it's progress. Maryam would love this."

Caleb followed his gaze, his expression unreadable. Then, without a word, he turned and began walking again. George lingered for a moment before following. The two men disappeared into the night as the light from the community center flickered and faded behind them.

Cedar Valley News Editorial
Confronting Crime in All Its Forms
By Samuel Tuttle, Senior Editor
Crime is a reality in Cedar Valley, as it is in every community. It's not a comfortable topic, but we must address it openly and honestly to protect our town and preserve the values that make it a strong, vibrant place to live. While recent tensions have put a spotlight on our new refugees neighbors, the facts show that crime in Cedar Valley is far more nuanced, with responsibility falling across various groups, including residents, migrant workers, illegal aliens, and outsiders.

First, let's clarify who these groups are and what they represent. The refugees who have arrived in Cedar Valley are not the same as migrant workers, immigrants who chose to voluntarily and safely leave their original country, or illegal aliens. The U.S. government thoroughly vetted these refugees and granted them legal status to settle here. Many of them worked alongside American troops in Afghanistan, risking their lives and livelihoods to support our country, and had to flee for their lives when the U.S. chaotically withdrew. They are doctors, teachers, mechanics, and laborers seeking to contribute and rebuild their lives. There is a very small percentage of Afghan refugees who are not in a family unit. An even smaller percentage of these individuals have problems adapting to our societal norms. The refugees brought to our town are specifically families. To equate them with other groups is not only unfair but also inaccurate.

Cedar Valley also has a population of migrant workers—individuals who move seasonally to work in industries like agriculture or construction. These workers are essential to many economies but, in some cases, have been associated with crime, notably when proper oversight and integration are lacking. Then there are illegal aliens, individuals who have entered or remained in the country unlawfully. By definition, their very presence constitutes a violation of the law, and some have been involved in criminal activities here in Cedar Valley. This is a reality we cannot ignore. While many illegal aliens are simply seeking better opportunities, a subset engages in serious offenses that harm communities and strain resources.

Outsiders, too, pose risks. Like many small towns, Cedar Valley has attracted individuals and groups who exploit its modest population and relative quiet for their own gain. Organized crime rings, opportunistic thieves, and fraudsters see towns like ours as easy targets. These groups are no less dangerous than any other criminal element, and their activities contribute significantly to the sense of unease that has gripped our community.

Finally, we must look inward. Cedar Valley's residents are not immune to committing crimes. Domestic disputes, theft, vandalism, and substance abuse have long been part of the town's challenges. To lay the blame for all our troubles at the feet of migrants, illegal aliens, or outsiders is to ignore the role that locals play in the crime we experience daily.

People of all ethnicities and walks of life get involved in crime. Acknowledging these distinct possible sources of criminal activities is crucial to solutions. We want a united community we must see the accurate picture and address the real problems. The Cedar Valley Police Department has repeatedly stated that the recent refugees are not connected to any rise in crime. These families are focused on building stable lives, not disrupting ours. Focusing on the other groups—migrants, illegal aliens, outsiders, and residents— rather than on the refugee families, will allow us to face this minor rise crime head-on.

So, where do we go from here? First, we must ensure that law enforcement has the tools and resources to address crime across all groups. This means targeting organized criminal activity from outsiders, addressing crimes committed by migrants or illegal aliens, and continuing to hold locals accountable for their actions. Chief Alan Brewster and his team have demonstrated a commitment to transparency and fairness, and their efforts deserve the community's full support.

Second, we need more vigorous oversight and integration programs for migrant workers to ensure they contribute positively to Cedar Valley without creating strain or conflict. These programs can help prevent the disconnect that leads to misunderstandings or, in some cases, crime.

Third, we must hold the federal government accountable for policies that contribute to the presence of illegal aliens. While many are here out of desperation, their unauthorized status creates an environment ripe for exploitation and lawlessness. As a town, we must advocate for solutions that balance compassion with the rule of law.

Finally, we must strengthen the ties that bind us as a community. Crime thrives in division, and spreading misinformation about one group or another only deepens the cracks in our foundation. Cedar Valley has always been a town that values neighborliness and unity. We cannot allow fear or falsehoods to strip us of that identity.

This is a challenging path forward, but it is necessary. Addressing crime in Cedar Valley cannot be done with blanket accusations or simplistic solutions. It requires a balanced approach—one that recognizes the nuances of our challenges and targets them with precision, fairness, and determination.

Cedar Valley is at a turning point. We can let fear divide us or rise to meet our challenges with clarity and resolve. Our immigrant neighbors, migrant workers, and even those here unlawfully represent different facets of the complex reality of modern life in small-town America. By addressing these challenges head-on, we can build a safer, stronger Cedar Valley—one that honors its values and the people who call it home.

A QUIET REFLECTION

Cedar Valley stood at the edge of change, its people grappling with truths that challenged long-held assumptions. George's reconciliation with his father reflected the power of forgiveness, a quiet but profound step toward healing fractures within families and the broader community. Despite societal expectations, his courage to support Aisha was a testament to bridges that could be built when compassion outweighed fear.

At the same time, Teresa's determination to confront misinformation illuminated a painful reality: division thrives when fear replaces understanding. Yet, amidst the skepticism and resistance, voices like Aisha's and Chloe's reminded the town of its shared humanity and the values that had long defined it. Caleb's quiet reflections and tentative steps toward empathy underscored the complexity of transformation—it was never easy, but it was possible.

The potluck dinner at the community center became a metaphor for what Cedar Valley could achieve. As neighbors shared food and stories, they found common ground in the simplest of moments. Distrust still lingered, but each act of kindness and courage brought the town closer to rediscovering its identity.

The path ahead was uncertain, but Cedar Valley's story wasn't over. In the delicate balance between neighbors and strangers lay the promise of unity—a quiet yet powerful tide, shifting ever so slowly toward hope.

CHAPTER 10

NEIGHBORS AND NEWCOMERS

The low hum of murmured conversations filled the town hall as Mayor Julia Randall approached the podium, her heels clicking softly against the wooden floor. The weight of the evening hung heavily in the room, and folding chairs packed with neighbors who once might have greeted each other warmly were now seated with arms crossed or expressions tight with concern. The ad-hoc community leaders sat in the first row. She placed her hands on the lectern, glanced over the faces before her, and began.

"Good evening, everyone. Thank you for taking the time to be here tonight. I know this meeting comes during a difficult time for Cedar Valley, and I deeply appreciate your commitment to our town and its future. We are a community that values honesty, hard work, and unity—and I believe those values brought each of you here tonight."

She paused, letting her words settle before continuing. "Over the past months, Cedar Valley has faced changes that have challenged all of us. The arrival of new residents—Afghan refugees who have joined our community—has stirred mixed emotions. Some of you feel hope and compassion, while others feel confusion, concern, and even fear. These reactions are valid, and our leaders and neighbors are responsible for addressing them openly and honestly."

Julia shifted slightly, her hands gripping the edges of the lectern. "There's been a lot of misinformation circulating about who these people are and why they're here, which has fueled misunderstandings and division in our community. But I believe Cedar Valley is stronger than that. We've always been a town that faces challenges together, and tonight, we begin that work." Teresa and Avery gave each other a knowing look. The work had been going on, the town's government just now joined. Finally.

She glanced toward the side of the stage where Chief Alan Brewster stood waiting. "To help us navigate these concerns and find a path forward, I've asked our police chief, Alan Brewster, to speak with us tonight. Chief Brewster has been working closely with his team to address the concerns many of you have raised and to clarify the issues at hand. I trust you'll give him your full attention as we build understanding and solutions. Chief Brewster, the floor is yours."

Chief Alan Brewster surveyed the packed town hall. The low hum of murmured conversations filled the space, a mix of frustration, curiosity, and unease that had become all too familiar in Cedar Valley. These were his people—neighbors he had known for decades, whose trust and respect he'd earned over 25 years of service. But tonight, many of them looked to him not as a familiar face but as the man they expected to provide answers to questions that had divided their once-close-knit town.

He adjusted the microphone and began. "Thank you all for coming tonight. I know this hasn't been an easy few months for Cedar Valley. We've seen big changes that have tested our patience, our resources, and, frankly, our understanding of one another. But before we get into tonight's discussion, I must clarify some confusion."

The room quieted as Brewster looked out over the crowd. "There's been a lot of talk about migrants, immigrants and refugees, and illegal aliens as if these terms are interchangeable. They're not. And we must understand the difference."

He paused, letting his words sink in. "The people who have recently arrived in Cedar Valley are immigrants. They've come here legally, vetted by the U.S. government, and most are families who worked alongside our troops in Afghanistan. These aren't people looking for handouts—they're here to work, rebuild their lives, and contribute to our community. They include doctors, lawyers, teachers, mechanics, and common laborers. But let's be clear—they are not migrant workers, who typically move from place to place for seasonal jobs, nor are they illegal aliens, individuals who entered the country without authorization."

A man near the back raised his hand. "But what about the crimes?" he asked, his tone skeptical. "You can't tell me there haven't been problems since they arrived."

Brewster nodded, acknowledging the question. "That's a fair concern, and I'm glad you brought it up. First, let's talk about Cedar Valley itself. Like any community, we've always had our share of crime—vandalism, theft, and even more serious incidents. These problems existed long before our new neighbors arrived. And while we've investigated every reported incident, we've found no evidence tying our immigrant community to any uptick in crime. Many of these rumors are baseless, fueled by misinformation intended to create fear and division."

He scanned the room, catching a few nods and more than a few skeptical frowns. "Now, I'm not saying there aren't challenges. Adjusting to such a significant population increase quickly isn't easy. Our schools are overcrowded, our healthcare system is stretched thin, and resources are being tested. These are real issues. But they're issues we can address together. What we can't afford to do is let misinformation cloud our judgment or allow outside forces to pit us against each other."

A woman in the front row stood, arms crossed. "If these people are so vetted and hardworking, why does it feel like the town is falling apart? We've got neighbors turning on each other, and now we're supposed to welcome strangers with open arms?"

Brewster's expression softened. "You're right. It does feel like the town is under strain. But let me ask you this—do you think it's the immigrants who are spreading those lies? Who's benefiting from neighbors turning on each other?" He stepped away from the lectern, his voice rising with passion. "These aren't organic problems. They're being fueled by organized groups—outsiders wanting to divide Cedar Valley. They thrive on chaos and use this situation to exploit our fears."

The woman didn't reply, but her arms slowly uncrossed, her posture relaxing slightly. Brewster continued, "And let's not forget who these people are. Many of them risked everything to stand by America. Ahmed, for example, served as an interpreter for our troops, risking his life every day to bridge the language gap in hostile territories. When the Taliban found out, they went after him and his family. He barely escaped with his life."

He gestured to a woman near the back. "Zahra worked as a medic in a U.S.-funded hospital, treating both Afghan civilians and American soldiers. When the hospital became a target, she smuggled critical supplies to keep patients alive, putting herself in constant danger. These people have come to Cedar Valley—not criminals, but allies who believed in America enough to stake their lives on it."

The room grew quieter, the tension shifting into something more thoughtful. A young man near the middle raised his hand. "But what about the strain on resources? My kids are in classrooms with 35 students, and it feels like the school can't handle it."

"That's a valid concern," Brewster replied. "Our schools are overcrowded, and that's something we're addressing. Superintendent Harris has contacted the state for additional funding to hire teachers and expand classroom space. We're also working with local nonprofits to provide extra support for students. It's not a quick fix, but we're making progress."

By the night's end, several residents had stepped forward to volunteer, adding their names to the sign-up sheets for various tasks at the back of the room. The tension that initially gripped the town hall had softened, replaced by cautious conversations and tentative nods of agreement.

As the last question was answered, Chief Brewster stepped back from the lectern, his steady demeanor giving way to a small, hopeful smile. He turned to Mayor Julia Randall, who stood nearby, observing the room with a thoughtful expression.

Taking her cue, Mayor Randall moved back to the lectern. She clasped her hands together, her voice steady as she addressed the crowd one last time. "Thank you all for coming tonight. We saw the first step in reclaiming the Cedar Valley we all know and love started by ground roots ad-hoc leaders," she motioned towards the group sitting in the front row.

"Before her tragic death, Maryam Khan was a key member of this group. Together we will regain our community of neighbors who care, listen, and act for the greater good."

She paused, looking out over the crowd. " It's time for government leadership to join the effort. Our challenges won't be solved overnight, but tonight, you've shown we can face them together. Thank you to those of you who volunteered. For those still unsure, I invite you to keep asking questions, engaging in these discussions, and, most importantly, showing up. Change is never easy, but it is possible, and I believe in Cedar Valley's ability to rise to this moment."

The mayor's words lingered in the air as she paused, her gaze sweeping across the room. "Let's keep this momentum going. You'll hear more from us in the coming weeks about how we can work together to address the issues we discussed tonight. For now, thank you for your time, your thoughts, and your commitment to our town."

As the crowd began to disperse, the room buzzed with quiet conversations. Chief Brewster exchanged handshakes with a few lingering residents while Mayor Randall approached the sign-up table, speaking briefly with volunteers who had offered their help. The weight of the evening hadn't lifted entirely, but it had shifted—no longer a suffocating burden but a challenge met with determination.

As the doors closed behind the last attendees, Mayor Randall and Chief Brewster exchanged glances. "A good meeting," she said, her tone firm and hopeful.

"Long road ahead," Brewster replied with a nod.

"Yes," she agreed, glancing toward the now-empty room. "But we're on it together. That's what matters."

Cedar Valley News
Residents Pack Town Hall to Address Community Tensions
By Sarah Whitman, Staff Reporter
Last night, the Cedar Valley Town Hall was standing-room-only as more than 200 residents gathered to address growing tensions in the community. Mayor Julia Randall called the

meeting to provide clarity and foster unity following months of the town government standing back as ad-hoc community leaders worked to resolve the division surrounding the arrival of immigrant families from Afghanistan.

The evening began with Mayor Randall delivering an impassioned speech that set a hopeful yet realistic tone. "The changes we've faced as a community have been challenging," she acknowledged. "But Cedar Valley has always been where neighbors come together, not drift apart. Tonight, I represent the local government joining the community leaders toward reclaiming that spirit."

Mayor Randall emphasized the importance of distinguishing between misinformation and legitimate concerns, clarifying that the town's newest residents are not migrants or illegal aliens but refugees who the U.S. government had vetted. Many of these families, she explained, worked alongside American troops in Afghanistan as interpreters, medics, and logistical support. "These families risked everything to stand with us," Randall stated. "Now, it's our turn to stand with them."

After her remarks, the mayor introduced Police Chief Alan Brewster, who addressed specific concerns raised by residents. Brewster's presentation focused on separating fact from fiction while acknowledging the strain the town has experienced. "Like any community, Cedar Valley has its challenges," he said. "But there is no evidence suggesting our new residents contribute to crime. Outside groups have spread many false rumors to divide us."

Chief Brewster also addressed concerns about the strain on local schools and healthcare systems, noting that proactive steps were underway. Superintendent Harris has secured additional funding from the state to expand classroom resources, and Dr. Aisha Khalid, a local healthcare provider, is collaborating with refugee professionals who have stepped up to assist with much-needed medical services.

The meeting was not without tension. Several residents voiced their frustrations, with one asking why the town should shoulder the burden of accommodating so many new families. Brewster's response was measured but firm. "This isn't just about resources," he said. "It's about who we are as a community. These families didn't just come here by chance—they came here because they believed in America's promise. We can choose to see them as a burden, or we can choose to see them as an opportunity to strengthen Cedar Valley."

The night's most poignant moment came when George Khan, a longtime Cedar Valley resident recently released from prison and working to rebuild his life, stood to speak. "I've spent years knowing what it's like to be judged unfairly," he shared. "I know what it feels like to be seen as an outsider, no matter how hard you try to move forward. But I also know what this town is capable of—kindness, acceptance, and second chances. Let's not lose sight of that."

By the end of the meeting, the tone in the room had shifted. Dozens of residents signed up to volunteer for new community initiatives, including cultural workshops and neighborhood outreach programs to build understanding between longtime residents and newcomers. While challenges remain, the meeting marked an important step toward bridging divides.

Speaking to reporters after the meeting, Mayor Randall expressed cautious optimism. "Tonight showed us what Cedar Valley can be when we listen to one another," she said. "We're far from finished, but I believe this is the beginning of a brighter chapter for our town."

For many residents, the meeting offered hope that Cedar Valley could progress. "It's about time we had this conversation," said a local hardware store owner, Lars Olson. "There's still work to do, but we're finally on the right track."

The next steps will include follow-up meetings and community projects to address the concerns raised. As Cedar Valley continues to navigate its challenges, last night's gathering demonstrated that the town's spirit of resilience and unity endures even in times of division.

A QUIET REFLECTION

The town hall's meeting was more than a gathering; it was a pivotal moment in Cedar Valley's journey toward rediscovering its identity. The voices raised—some filled with skepticism, others with hope—reflected the delicate balance of fear and possibility that defined the community. Mayor Randall's call for clarity and Chief Brewster's unwavering focus on truth illuminated the path forward, even as obstacles loomed.

George Khan's words resonated deeply, a reminder that judgment and division could be overcome by compassion and second chances. His own story stood as proof that individuals and communities could change when given the opportunity. The residents who signed up to volunteer and engage in cultural workshops showed that the seeds of understanding were beginning to take root despite lingering doubts.

Cedar Valley's challenges were far from over, but the meeting marked a critical shift. It was a moment of recognition—not just of the difficulties ahead but of the shared strength that could overcome them. As neighbors and newcomers started to see each other as people rather than stereotypes, a quiet echo of hope began to ripple through the town, whispering of a future built on trust, empathy, and unity.

CHAPTER 11
REBUILDING TOGETHER

The community health clinic bustled with activity as Chloe stepped through the door, balancing a tray of freshly baked muffins in one hand and a box of pamphlets in the other. Aisha looked up from the reception desk, a tired but genuine smile on her face.

"Chloe! You're a lifesaver," Aisha said, stepping around the desk to help her.

"I thought these might help keep everyone energized," Chloe said, setting the muffins on the counter. She glanced at the crowded waiting area, filled with a mix of familiar Cedar Valley faces and newcomers still finding their place in the town.

Over the past few weeks, Chloe had spent more and more time at the clinic. At first, she had hesitated, worried she might not be helpful. But Aisha's quiet encouragement and the sense of purpose she felt while working there quickly erased her doubts.

"Can you help with the registration table?" Aisha asked, nodding toward a makeshift setup near the door.

Chloe nodded and took her place behind the table, greeting each person with a smile as they approached. She listened to their stories—mothers worried about their children's health, fathers looking for job resources, teenagers dreaming of college. Each interaction deepened her understanding of the community and strengthened her resolve to make a difference.

When the clinic wound down for the day, Chloe felt a quiet satisfaction settle over her. She hadn't solved all the town's problems, but she had taken a step—a small but meaningful step—toward being the person she wanted to be.

As she helped Aisha clean up, Chloe caught her reflection in the clinic's glass door. She looked the same as she had a few months ago, but something had shifted inside her. She wasn't just watching Cedar Valley change anymore; she was part of the change.

George Khan sat on the familiar, slightly worn couch in his parents' living room, leaning forward with his elbows on his knees. His father, Ahmed, sat across from him in his favorite armchair, the lines on his face deepened by months of stress and inactivity. Though the room was quiet, unspoken thoughts hung heavy between them. George broke the silence.

"Dad," he began, his tone careful but firm, "now that the insurance money has come in from the fire, what do you think about starting construction on the deli?"

Ahmed, staring absently at the carpet, lifted his eyes to his son. His brow furrowed, and he shifted uncomfortably in his chair. "But the site isn't ready for construction," he said at last. "It's a big expense to clean it up."

George nodded, expecting this answer. "I know. But what if we didn't have to do it all ourselves? We could ask Dan Larson to organize a work party of volunteers. We could hire some of the heavy stuff out, but most of it... most of it could be a community project."

Ahmed raised an eyebrow. "A community project?"

"Yeah," George said, leaning forward with growing enthusiasm. "We could get residents and refugees working together. Think about it, Dad. It could bring people closer. And it wouldn't just be about rebuilding the deli—it'd be about rebuilding this town."

Later that evening, the Khan family gathered in the living room for prayer. Ahmed led the prayer, his voice low and measured, while George, his sister Fatima, and his aunt Jamila sat in a semicircle, murmuring their fervent intentions.

For George, prayer brought a moment of clarity. The deli wasn't just a business to his family—it was a legacy crafted lovingly by his late sister, Maryam. Her influence was everywhere: in the recipes she'd perfected, the warm community she'd fostered, and even in the layout of the building itself. Ahmed sat back in his chair as the family finished their prayer, sighing deeply.

"Where do we start?" Ahmed asked, his voice heavy with emotion. "Where do we start now, son?"

George paused, the weight of his father's question settling over him. "If you recall, she never used the entire floor," he said, his tone thoughtful. "The room beside her office—she mostly used it for storage. It's just sitting there, full of junk. We could clear it out and repurpose it."

Ahmed nodded slowly, but there was hesitation in his eyes. "And what would we do with it?"

George hesitated, but then his voice grew stronger. "We use it to expand on what Maryam started. I remember she always wanted to expand the Deli someday. We can honor all that, including her menus, generosity, and willingness to try new things. We need to expand it."

"She did want to do that. But you make it sound simple, son," Ahmed said, though his tone showed a glimmer of interest. "Please, continue with your line of thought. I'm still at a loss, but your words encourage me."

The words struck George deeply. His father's admission erased years of distance and isolation between them, filling him with unexpected emotion. "I have more ideas," George said, his voice steady despite the lump in his throat. "We should memorialize her—her vision, courage, faith. We could make this deli something bigger. Something that brings the community together."

"Keep going, son. You have my attention," Ahmed said.

"First, we keep the menu the same," George began, leaning forward. "That's what everyone loves—our regulars will want that sense of continuity. But what if we added something new? Something different. We could convert that storage room into an Afghan-run ethnic deli."

Ahmed's eyes widened, his mouth falling open. "An Afghan deli? George, that could ruin everything!"

"No, Dad," George replied, his tone rising with conviction. "Think about it. Maryam took risks all the time. Remember when she started introducing Pakistani spices to the menu? People said it wouldn't work. But she believed in it—and it did work. This would be the same idea. It's not just about food. It's about showing Cedar Valley that we're all in this together."

Ahmed's gaze softened as he considered his son's words. "You're right," he admitted quietly. "Maryam always dared to take chances, especially helping the refugees despite community distrust. And she always believed in giving back to others."

"Exactly," George said, seizing the momentum. "We owe it to her to keep that spirit alive. And we already have the resources—an extra sink, a second oven, plenty of kitchen space. It's just sitting there, waiting for us to do something with it."

Ahmed sighed, a mix of doubt and admiration flickering across his face. "You're asking a lot, son. But I can see that you believe in this. And... maybe it's time we did something bold."

The next day, George began spreading the word. His first call was to Dan Larson, who immediately offered his support. "A cleanup day?" Dan repeated, his voice crackling over the line. "I'll have a crew ready by Saturday."

By the weekend, volunteers flooded the deli site. Refugees and locals worked side by side, hauling debris and sorting salvaged materials. Caleb Mercer, now a steady presence in the community, coordinated efforts with precision, translating between English and Dari as he directed teams of workers.

Ahmed, who had planned to watch from the sidelines, soon found himself in the thick of it. He worked alongside an Afghan carpenter to assess the space's potential, while George collaborated with the younger volunteers to clear the storage room. The site began transforming as the sun dipped lower, casting long shadows across the lot.

"What do you think, Dad?" George asked, gesturing toward the cleared-out space.

Ahmed surveyed the scene, his expression a mix of pride and nostalgia. "It's starting to feel like home again."

As the cleanup wrapped up, George gathered the volunteers for a quick meeting. Standing atop a makeshift platform, he raised his voice to address the group.

"This deli isn't just about food," he began, with Caleb translating for the Afghans in the crowd. "It's about community. About honoring the people who came before us—like my sister, Maryam—and creating something new for the future. Together, we're not just rebuilding a business. We're rebuilding Cedar Valley."

The crowd erupted in applause, their cheers echoing across the lot. Ahmed, standing beside his son, placed a hand on his shoulder. "You've done something special here," he said quietly. "Your mother and sister would be proud."

George's throat tightened, but he managed a smile. "Thanks, Dad. But we're just getting started." The Khans gathered for another prayer at the family home that evening. This time, their words were filled with gratitude and hope. As Ahmed closed the prayer, he turned to his son with a rare warmth in his eyes.

"You've taught me something today, George," he said. "Faith isn't just about worship. It's about action—about taking risks and trusting the people around you."

George nodded; his heart full. "And it's about doing it together."

☐ A QUIET REFLECTION

Rebuilding is never just about structures; it's about people—about the stories, values, and dreams they carry. For George and Ahmed Khan, the decision to rebuild the deli was more than a practical undertaking; it was a way to honor Maryam's vision and the indelible mark she left on Cedar Valley. Her courage to take risks and her unwavering generosity became the foundation upon which their renewed purpose was built.

As refugees and long-time residents worked side by side to clear the site, the boundaries that once divided them began to blur. Caleb's steady leadership and Dan's rallying of volunteers showed how collaboration could transform hesitation into hope. The cleanup day was not only about physical labor; it was a testament to the strength found in unity, where cultural and personal differences became a source of inspiration rather than division.

In those moments, Cedar Valley felt its heart beating again, not only in the debris being cleared or the tools being wielded, but in the shared laughter, exchanged stories, and the quiet understanding that rebuilding the deli was also rebuilding the town. Faith and action, once distant ideas, now moved hand in hand, reminding everyone involved that true transformation comes when hope is shared, risks are embraced, and progress is made—together.

CHAPTER 12
SEEDS OF PURPOSE

C aleb Mercer stood a little apart from people leaving the meeting, arms crossed and brow furrowed. The latest meeting had been a promising one, he admitted to himself. More and more people were turning toward helping the refugees, breaking down barriers, and forming connections. But a nagging thought gnawed at him as he watched his neighbors express their optimism.

What about their own people, he thought to himself. Caleb's life had been on a steady decline for months. Laid off from his job and struggling to find new work, he had spent countless nights wrestling with feelings of frustration and bitterness. Did anyone in this town care about the residents like him, the ones who were falling through the cracks?

Walking home alone that night, Caleb couldn't hold back the question that had been burning inside him. "God, do You care?" he whispered into the darkness. "If You do, please talk to me. I must know."

When he reached his apartment, the silence was a relief. His wife wasn't home—likely out looking for work herself. Caleb sat down heavily in his favorite chair and reached for his Bible. "God, please, speak to me," he prayed. "Show me what makes George so dedicated to You. I need to understand."

He flipped through the pages aimlessly, the weight of the thick book a reminder of how little he knew where to start. Frustration boiled over as the Bible slipped from his hands, landing on the floor with a heavy thud. His eyes fell on the open page as he bent to pick it up. It was the Gospel of John, chapter one. With a deep breath, Caleb began to read. Hours passed as he moved through the text, his heart softening with every verse.

"Jesus, Jesus, I believe," he whispered at last, tears streaming down his face. "Please make me a sheep in Your fold." For the first time in months, Caleb felt a sense of peace.

The next day, Caleb joined the group in a meeting room at the Community Center . A newfound resolve steadied him.

Last night's meeting itself had been spirited—sometimes tense—but there was an undeniable sense that something was shifting in Cedar Valley. The group, a mix of long-time residents and newer arrivals, gathered to distill what had been said and what still needed to be done. Caleb's renewed faith gave him new inspiration to help towards community unity.

Teresa Nikas, ever the historian, was the first to speak. Her straight black hair in a ponytail swung as she tilted her head thoughtfully. "Since its founding, Cedar Valley has been a lumber town," she began, her voice measured. "The International Paper Company ran everything—logging, wood processing, the mills. Sure, it brought jobs but also a lot of noise and some new health problems. Over the years, those industries faded, and we became quieter. Quieter but emptier too. With this shift toward retail and tourism, we're a different place—a pleasant, quiet echo of what we used to be."

Aisha said, "Thank you for the history summary. It's been loud again recently. Not just actual noise but emotional noise. Ever since the refugees came, it felt like people were shouting at each other. Resentment, frustration, fear—it was overwhelming. But something's changed. The noise is quieting. I feel it in myself. People are starting to accept each other."

Caleb Mercer lingered a little further back from the group. The group's optimism grated against the frustration still simmering in him. He reminded himself of the peace he had felt last night, which lowered the temperature of his words. "You think another food event is gonna fix this? he asked, breaking the lull in the conversation. His tone had a rough edge, though not an unkind one. He looked at Aisha and Dan Larson, his frustration evident. "People don't change just because they share a meal."

"No," Aisha admitted, her voice soft but steady, "that is where we started, and you have to admit it has made a difference.."

Caleb shook his head, pacing a few steps away. His hands stayed buried in his coat pockets, fists clenched. He muttered. "It's not enough. Charity isn't enough." He turned back toward them, his expression tightening into determination. "What if... what if we did something bigger? Not just charity, but build on the fragile connection."

Dan, thoughtful as ever, raised an eyebrow. "Like what?"

Caleb hesitated, the words catching in his throat before they tumbled out. "A community skills exchange. Build on the few classes the county's initiative covers. On the Afghan's trades, what drove their economy, our trades, like carpentry. . Everyone brings something and learns something. Just people helping each other, learning from each other, respecting each person's values."

For a moment, there was silence. The click of the clock was the the only sound. Aisha was the first to break the silence, her eyes bright with understanding. "Mutual investment," she said, her voice rising with enthusiasm. "Shared stakes. That's what this town needs. We've started something similar with the Medical Administration Taskforce I'm leading."

Dan nodded slowly, his brow furrowed as he considered the idea. "Might make folks see each other as more than just headlines and rumors."

Caleb met their gazes, his expression steady and resolved. "We can create workshops on various skills, basically a trade school." Aisha extended her hand toward him. "Let's do it."

Dan reached out, clasping both their hands with a firm grip. "We will do this," his voice encouraged, "and we will do it right."

Caleb felt something stir inside him in that moment—a sense of purpose he hadn't felt since losing his factory job. He wasn't just watching or reacting to the changes in Cedar Valley; he was shaping them.

Chloe Papadakis, who had quietly listened to the exchange, nodded in agreement. "I share your sentiment," she said passionately. "I see it too. It's not just about avoiding conflict anymore—it's about embracing something new. The other night, I heard music in the square—Afghan songs mingling with folk tunes. It was so beautiful, so... connected. I feel like Cedar Valley is finding a new harmony."

The group fell silent again, reflecting on Chloe's words. The idea of harmony struck a chord. For months, Cedar Valley had been a town fighting dissonance, its people struggling to reconcile their differences. But now, there was a sense that those differences could become something more—a shared rhythm, a new song.

George Khan, seated in a chair by the door, raised his hand hesitantly. "Can I say something?" he asked, though his excitement was already apparent.

"Of course," Dan replied, smiling warmly.

George took a deep breath before speaking. "—I was thinking I never would have a second chance with my family or this town. . But now, I'm reconciled with my family including Maryam before we lost her, and I feel like people are moving towards accepting both the newcomers and me. There's a sense of positivity, of freedom. People are starting to treat each other with respect, and that's... that's everything. It feels good." He continued, "As you know, my family is rebuilding the Deli Kitchen, and expanding it to include Afghan ethnic food. Regarding what you are saying, Caleb, we want to use both new and old menus to bring newcomers and 'old' residents together, rebuilding the community atmosphere of our Deli Kitchen that Maryam loved so much."

His words hung in the air; their sincerity unmistakable. For George, who had often felt out of step in Cedar Valley since his release from jail, this newfound harmony was a relief, a balm for the uncertainty he had carried for so long.

Teresa spoke again, focusing less on the past and more on the possibilities ahead. "We've been through so much change, which hasn't been easy. But maybe that's what makes it worth it. We need to fight through the noise, the tension, the differences—it's a sign that we're alive and growing. And growth is never quiet."

Aisha leaned forward, her eyes shining with determination. "I love that your family is rebuilding the Deli Kitchen bringing back the unity Maryam cherished. So, what do we do next? How do we keep this momentum going?"

Dan nodded. "These are great ideas, a trade school, and the way the Khan's are rebuilding their Deli Kitchen. . And we could involve the high school students in the planning as well, they enjoyed participating in the Community Fair. They're the future, after all."

Standing beside her husband, Rebecca Larson added, "And we'll need to make sure everyone feels included—new families, old families, everyone. That's how we make this stick."

Caleb grinned, the earlier tension in his posture replaced by hope. "Sounds like we've got a plan."

☐ A QUIET REFLECTION

The seeds of purpose had been planted in Cedar Valley, but their growth depended on more than goodwill—it required trust, collaboration, and a willingness to see one another as equals. Caleb's newfound resolve, shaped by frustration and faith, symbolized a turning point. His idea of a skills exchange wasn't just about learning trades; it was about learning to respect and rely on one another, breaking down the barriers that had long divided the town.

A shared rhythm began to emerge in the voices of Aisha, Chloe, George, and the others. The dissonance that once defined Cedar Valley was transforming into harmony, each voice adding to a new melody of hope. It wasn't perfect, and tensions still simmered beneath the surface, but for the first time in months, the community felt united in pursuing something greater than its fears.

As ideas flowed and plans formed, a quiet determination settled over the group. This wasn't just about patching cracks or mending what was broken—it was about building something new, something stronger. The skills exchange, the cultural fair, and the involvement of the town's youth all pointed to a future where Cedar Valley's differences became its strength.

In the quiet of that moment, under the fading light of the day, the town's collective heartbeat grew steadier. Cedar Valley was finding its purpose, one conversation, one act of courage, and one shared dream at a time.

CHAPTER 13
MIDNIGHT ECHOES

I t happened just around midnight. The sound was unmistakably an explosion, jarring the sleepy town from its slumber. The blast echoed through the narrow streets scattering debris, a thunderous roar that rolled over the darkened houses and spilled into the surrounding hills. In its wake came a ringing silence that made even the crickets go quiet.

The bomb had gone off near the community hall, the same place where a contentious town meeting had recently been held. By the end of it, it led to calming fears and encouraging many to move toward unity. Volunteers signed up to plan events that encouraged one joined community. . It didn't take long for the residents of Cedar Valley to connect the dots. This wasn't a random act of violence. Someone—or perhaps several someones—had made their dissatisfaction with the growing peace known in the most destructive way possible.

By dawn, the town was abuzz with speculation. Groups gathered outside coffee shops, on porches, and in the town square, their voices low but intense. Theories flourished like weeds. Was it another protest against the influx of refugees? A warning for the ad-hoc leaders to stop their efforts? A backlash to Mayor Julia Randall's call for unity? Or was it simply the act of a troubled individual lashing out at a changing world they couldn't control?

In his cramped office on the second floor of the police station, Chief Brewster surveyed the scene below through a streaked window. His desk was cluttered with papers, a half-empty coffee cup, and a police scanner that crackled intermittently. The explosion had left a small crater near the back of the community hall, shattering windows and charring the nearby grass. Miraculously, no one had been hurt, but the psychological damage was more challenging to quantify.

Mayor Julia Randall arrived mid-morning, her face pale and drawn. "What do we know?" she asked as she stepped into Chief Brewster's office.

Chief Brewster gestured toward the window. "Not much yet. Forensics is working on it, it looks like a homemade device. Small, but enough to make a statement."

Julia frowned, crossing her arms. "A statement? About what? The recent town hall?"

"Probably," Chief Brewster replied. He leaned back in his chair, the leather creaking under his weight. "But it wasn't the work of a group. This was one person, maybe two at most."

Julia raised an eyebrow. "You're sure?"

"Pretty sure." Chief Brewster scratched his chin thoughtfully. "Historically, when you've got a big, angry crowd, you get riots—lots of violence all at once. But this? This is a lone wolf. Someone with a grudge, too afraid to show his face."

"Or her face," Julia cut in.

Chief Brewster nodded. "Could be. Doesn't change much. Lone wolves don't tend to repeat themselves if they think everyone's against them. They don't want to be outcasts. As long as the community condemns this—and I mean everyone—we won't see another bomb."

The immediate response to the bombing was one of outrage and condemnation. Mayor Randall took to the airwaves that afternoon, delivering a firm statement from the town hall steps before the broadcast media. "This act of violence does not represent Cedar Valley," she declared, her voice steady despite the tremor in her hands. "We will not let fear dictate our actions or divide our community. We are moving towards being a welcoming, generous community again, and we won't stop now."

For some, her words were a comfort. For others, they rang hollow. Whispers spread through the town—questions about whether the refugees had brought trouble with them or whether the mayor's push for inclusivity had gone too far. Conversations turned tense in the small diner on Main Street as long-time residents argued over the attack's implications.

"I told you this would happen," someone muttered. "Bringing in all those outsiders—it's just asking for trouble."

"You don't know that it was them," countered Teresa Nikas, who had become one of the refugees' staunchest advocates. "It could've been anyone."

"You don't think it's suspicious, all these problems cropping up since they arrived?"

Teresa's face flushed with anger. "The only problem here is people like you, People who'd rather point fingers than fix anything."
Chief Brewster watched the rising tensions with a wary eye. Though the community seemed united in condemning the bombing, underlying divisions were still there. His small team of officers worked tirelessly to piece together evidence, but progress was slow; they had never dealt with such a crime before. Additionally, whoever had planted the bomb had been careful, leaving behind few clues.

In the meantime, Chief Brewster made it his mission to keep the peace. He walked the streets daily, calming a town teetering on the edge of discord. At every turn, he reminded people to rebuild trust and ensure everyone felt safe.

One evening, as Chief Brewster patrolled the town square, he spotted Caleb Mercer lingering near the newly erected barricades around the community hall. Caleb's expression was hard to read, a mixture of frustration and resolve.

"You doing okay?" Brewster asked, stopping beside him.

Caleb hesitated before replying. "I don't know. I thought we were making progress. After the meeting, I really believed people were starting to come together. And then this happens."

Brewster nodded; his gaze fixed on the damaged building. "Change isn't easy, Caleb. But it's worth fighting for. Whoever did this wants us to lose faith in each other. Don't let them win."

Caleb seemed to consider this, his shoulders relaxing slightly. "You think we'll find them?"

"We will," Chief Brewster said firmly. "And when we do, we'll show them this town is stronger than their hate."

Despite the fear and uncertainty after the initial shock, Cedar Valley's residents refused to be cowed. In the days following the bombing, acts of kindness and solidarity emerged. A group of volunteers gathered to repair the damage to the community hall, their efforts drawing onlookers who soon joined in. Refugee families worked alongside long-time residents, their shared labor a quiet defiance against the violence that had sought to divide them.

Dr. Aisha Khalid, one of the most vocal advocates for unity, organized a candlelight vigil in the town square. The event drew a diverse crowd, their faces illuminated by the soft glow of hundreds of candles. Standing at the center of the gathering, Aisha addressed the crowd with quiet conviction.

"This attack was meant to scare us, to make us turn against each other," she said. "But tonight, we stand together to say no. Cedar Valley is a place where everyone belongs. And we won't let hate take that away."

Her words were met with applause, the sound echoing through the square like a promise. For many, the vigil was a turning point—a reminder that the community's strength lay in its unity.

Behind the scenes, Chief Brewster and his team worked tirelessly to unravel the mystery of the bombing. The breakthrough came nearly two weeks later when a fragment of the explosive device was traced to a local hardware store. Surveillance footage showed a lone figure purchasing the materials—a man in his early thirties, wearing a baseball cap and sunglasses.

The suspect, identified as Tim Rourke, was a former resident of Cedar Valley who had left town years earlier under murky circumstances.

He had returned only recently, staying in a rundown motel on the outskirts of town. When officers searched his room, they found incriminating evidence: blueprints of the community hall, handwritten notes detailing the town meeting, and a half-assembled explosive device.

Chief Brewster confronted Rourke in the interrogation room, his demeanor calm but firm. "Why'd you do it, Tim?"

Rourke sneered, his defiance thinly masking his fear. "You people don't get it, do you? You're letting them take over—changing everything."

"'Them'?" Brewster repeated. "You mean the refugees?"

Rourke didn't answer, but the silence was enough. Chief Brewster leaned forward, his voice low and steady. "You've got it wrong, Tim. They aren't taking over Cedar Valley. It's changing because townspeople and Afghan refugees are choosing hope over fear. You tried to stop that, but you only made us stronger."

Rourke scoffed. "You've also made crime stronger." Realizing he hadn't meant to give that away, he stopped talking.

Intrigued, Chief Brewster leaned forward. "What are you talking about."

Cursing under his breath at blurting out the truth he hadn't meant to share, Rourke looked at the ceiling, considering if he would continue. "If I tell you what I know, will it help me in the fix I've gotten myself in?"

Chief Brewster already knew he wanted a deal. "I will talk to the prosecutor; he has to decide."

Rourke considered for another moment, then shrugged his shoulders. "Might as well keep talking." He settled back in his chair. "You got the refugee families living in Cedar Valley. Even the single Afghan refugee men say their decent folk. Most of those guys are decent, too. There are a few who are not. They want to exploit the defenseless. They find plenty in the cities, more opportunity, you know what I mean," he said sarcastically. "You know they are out there."

"Yes, we do. We find them eventually and put them where they belong: jail."

"Well, there's a small gang, just a few, who stay in one of the hotels and keep to themselves. They leave for a few days and return better off than they were. A time or two, they've added a new member. All the refugees are afraid of them, and they demand subordinate respect from everyone, me and my associates included. We don't like it, but something about them, their eyes." He paused.

Pulling out his pen and notepad, Chief Brewster asked, "Do you know any of their names? Do you know where they go?"

After another minute, considering what more to reveal, he continued. "I really mean it when I say they are scary dudes. Back in the city, some bad things happened; I suspect they know something about disappearances and, worse, refugees' deaths."

Startled, Chief Brewster looked up. "What do you know about possible murders in those cities?" He was very intent on the turn taken in the interrogation.

"I don't know details; of course, I don't know what they are saying! I only understand the looks of their faces, and they carry serious weapons. Honestly, I don't look them in the eye and hope they don't look at me either. I came back here to get away from that danger unease. But then I see them here. They are here too?! So yes, the refugees are changing everything! And you all are helping them! Rourke returned to his sullen attitude and said nothing else.

Chief Brewster put his notepad away. "We are determined to make this change to include the newcomers positive, and bring to justice the criminals like you've described."

"Don't forget criminals like me, too!" Rourke said morosely, leading the police chief to believe he regretted his destructive decision to cause a dangerous explosion.

With Rourke in custody, the immediate threat to Cedar Valley was removed. But the scars of the bombing remained, both physical and emotional. The community hall, though repaired, bore a faint burn mark on its rear wall—a reminder of the night that had tested the town's resolve.

For Julia Randall, the incident was a call to action. She doubled down on her efforts to bridge the divides within Cedar Valley, launching new programs to foster dialogue and collaboration. The skills exchange initiative, already gaining traction, expanded to include mentorship opportunities, pairing long-time residents with refugee families to share knowledge and build relationships.

Caleb Mercer, inspired by Chief Brewster's words and the resilience of his neighbors, threw himself into the town's rebuilding efforts. He became a familiar figure at the community hall, organizing events and encouraging others to get involved. Most important, after renewing his relationship with his Lord, he knew he needed and wanted to renew the relationship with his wife. She deserved so much better than what he was giving rather than not giving. First of all, he began therapy as she had been begging him to for a long time.

Months later, as spring bloomed in Cedar Valley, the town gathered again in the square. This time, it was not to mourn or protest but to celebrate. A new mural adorned the side of the community hall, a project lead by Teresa and Avery, its vibrant colors depicting the diverse faces of the town's residents, old and new. Beneath it, a plaque read: "In Unity, We Thrive."

Chief Brewster stood at the crowd's edge, watching Mayor Randall take the stage to address the gathering. Her voice rang out clear and confident, a far cry from the shaken mayor who had addressed the town months earlier. .

"Tonight, we celebrate not just what we've overcome but what we've built together," she said. "And together, we will continue to make Cedar Valley better."

The crowd erupted into applause, their cheers filling the air like a promise. Cedar Valley had faced its darkest hour and emerged stronger; its people were bound by a shared determination to create a community where everyone could belong. Chief Brewster listened to the meeting, pleased with the progress. The County Law Enforcement Taskforce was making great strides in lowering crime, including solving serious crimes using clues Rourke provided. Despite his help, Rourke was facing serious time for the bombing. As the Chief looked at the faces before him, he knew the town's best days were still ahead.

A QUIET REFLECTION

The midnight explosion shattered more than the quiet of Cedar Valley—
it threatened the fragile trust that the town had begun to rebuild. Yet,
something remarkable emerged as the dust settled and the shock subsid-
ed. Despite their differences, the people of Cedar Valley chose to confront
the act of violence not with division but with determination to unite.

The bombing was a stark reminder of the lingering fears and tensions that had shadowed the community. But it also became a catalyst
for change. George's quiet strength, Caleb's resilience, Aisha's unwavering
advocacy, and Brewster's steady leadership reflected the town's capacity to
rise above hatred and suspicion. Each voice and action carried the weight
of defiance against the forces that sought to fracture their home.

The candlelight vigil, the shared labor to repair the hall, and the
mural that now adorned its walls were more than symbolic—they were
tangible expressions of Cedar Valley's refusal to be defined by fear. They
whispered a truth that echoed through the town: unity is not the absence
of conflict but the choice to face it together.

Cedar Valley's journey was continuing, though the scars, both visible
and unseen, remained. But in every act of kindness and every step toward
understanding, the community reclaimed its identity. They were not a town
divided—they were neighbors rebuilding, one quiet echo of hope at a time.

CHAPTER 14
FROM FRACTURES TO FOUNDATIONS

The bombing that threatened to disrupt Cedar Valley's journey toward unity ultimately proved something remarkable: the number of individuals inclined toward violence was extraordinarily small—it had been an isolated, singular act. While tensions lingered, the bombing underscored a key truth about the community. Acceptance was growing, even if grudgingly at times. Living alongside those who differed—in culture, background, or belief—was becoming the norm. Violence and hate offered no path forward. The perpetrator of the bombing, a disgruntled outsider, had failed to leave a lasting mark, and his arrest contributed to decreasing the discord on the road leading inevitably toward understanding. Cedar Valley's story is not one of perfection but progress, where neighbors grappled with change and found ways to move forward—together.

Cedar Valley's community hall had become the beating heart of the town, a revitalized space buzzing with energy and purpose. Its vivid mural—a celebration of the town's diverse faces—had quickly transformed into a symbol of unity. The mural wasn't just admired; it was loved, a gathering place where neighbors lingered over cups of coffee from the nearby deli, exchanging stories and laughter. Gradually, the impromptu social corner outside the hall grew, with tables, chairs, pots of flowers, and even umbrellas appearing as if by magic, each addition a testament to the community's renewed spirit.

Caleb paused outside the community hall, where warm light spilled from the windows, casting a welcoming glow against the cool spring evening. Inside, laughter and conversation hummed, the air alive with purpose as neighbors worked together, packing care boxes and sorting donations.

"It feels like winter doesn't want to let go and let spring in!" Caleb remarked as he stepped inside, shaking off the chill. The warmth hit him not only from the heaters but also from the shared camaraderie of the space where the townspeople were rebuilding something lasting.

"Caleb! Over here!" Aisha Khalid's voice called out, her smile radiant as she waved him over to a table stacked with supplies.

He joined her, nodding at the buzz of activity. "Busy night."

"The best kind," Aisha replied with a determined glint in her eye. "We've come a long way."

"It's been feeling different," Caleb mused. ". We are helping and building something real."

Aisha met his gaze, her tone steady. "We are. One step at a time."

Across the hall, George Khan watched the interaction with a small smile. He couldn't help but marvel at the change. He felt it in the steady hum of his family's deli, the camaraderie of the workshops at the hall, and most profoundly during his family prayers. He felt a sense of belonging in Cedar Valley—a belonging nurtured first by being restored to his family and then by the friendships he was cultivating. Dan's mentorship gave him spiritual guidance. His and Caleb's camaraderie grew, having the traits of resilience and a natural aptitude for blue-collar work. Their complex personalities gave them an unspoken brotherhood. He was proud he was among the first residents, the ad-hoc leaders, who were compelled to get Cedar Valley on its journey to unity. But with her elegance and quiet strength, Aisha Khalid had stirred something deeper. She was kindness personified, coaxing smiles and inspiring confidence with every gesture. Around her, George found himself striving—to dress better, to stand taller, to be more.

At the community workshops, Aisha and George saw each other often. George worked with the men, guiding them through hands-on projects in an easygoing manner, with Caleb translating. They laughed together at the occasional language stumbles. Aisha took the women under her wing into her kitchen. Making cultural dishes filled the air with tantalizing spices, each aroma an unspoken promise of the feast to come. The energy was infectious, and each success was celebrated with smiles and shared stories.

Despite his growing confidence, George felt vulnerable around Aisha. Still, he planned to ask her for help with a new Afghan menu for the deli, blending her natural understanding of the refugees' culture with her culinary finesse. Caleb, who also struggled with feelings of isolation, was the perfect ally to help embolden George to ask for Aisha's help. George and Caleb were determined to build up each other's confidence and resilience. Together, the three of them could transform the spare deli room into a vibrant new space to restore the community atmosphere Maryam had nurtured for years.

One day, as the lunch hour arrived, George, in his haste to fetch more plates, collided headlong into Aisha in the bustling kitchen. The resulting chaos sent food flying, drawing gasps and then peals of laughter as George caught Aisha mid-stumble. Their faces were inches apart, their expressions frozen in surprise before they both burst into laughter, their joy rippling through the room. Even as they cleaned up the mess, their shared smiles lingered—a quiet echo of something unspoken.

George watched the community hall buzz with life inside the workshops. He felt a quiet contentment, knowing that amidst the laughter and shared work, he and Aisha were building something far more significant than they realized—both for the town and, perhaps, for each other.

Cedar Valley's transformation reached its pinnacle at the town's Gala, a grand event promoted by Mayor Randall to celebrate the community's progress.

The hall buzzed with life as locals and visitors gathered for food, music, and dance. Aisha and Owen invited Fatima to play the sitar as they performed traditional Pakistani and Afghani folk dances, captivating the crowd with grace and cultural storytelling.

Nearby, Teresa and Chloe shared the history of Cedar Valley, highlighting the courage and resilience of longtime residents and new refugees. Lars Olson demonstrated carpentry and other skills, inviting participants to try their hand at trades essential to rebuilding homes and lives.

Dan and Rebecca brought playful energy to the event with their obstacle course and the Gala Challenge, a series of whimsical games that delighted participants of all ages. Young and old competed in ten events, including the paper plate discus throw, whiffle ball shot put, plastic straw javelin throw, high jump, water jump, belly crawl, rubber band shot, ape-man walk, egg balance, and tightrope traverse. Laughter and cheers echoed as families and friends tried their hand at each challenge, creating memories that would last well beyond the event.

Chief Brewster wandered through the hall, nodding to neighbors and exchanging smiles. Charmed by the festivities, visitors from other towns spoke eagerly of Cedar Valley's transformation. Some even approached Mayor Randall to learn more, hinting that the town's burgeoning unity might soon become a beacon for others.

George, Caleb, and Aisha stood together, watching the crowd mingle. It felt like Cedar Valley's fractures were genuinely beginning to heal—one step, one shared laugh, and one quiet echo at a time.

Cedar Valley News

Residents Honored for Welcoming Spirit Toward Refugees

By Sarah Whitman, Staff Reporter

In a heartfelt ceremony at Cedar Valley's bustling community hall, Mayor Julia Randall and Police Chief Allan Brewster recognized several residents for their extraordinary efforts in welcoming Afghan refugees to the town. These individuals, nominated by their neighbors, received Certificates of Recognition for their dedication to fostering kindness, understanding, and integration into one community for Cedar Valley. "Cedar Valley has proven what's possible when a community works together," Mayor Randall remarked. "While larger cities have struggled with refugee resettlement, our town is a beacon of collaboration and compassion. These honorees have not only changed lives but also strengthened the fabric of our community." These are the honorees, spanning diverse professions and backgrounds, who were celebrated for their impactful contributions:

Teresa Nikas
A beloved high school teacher, Teresa has become a symbol of hope and leadership in Cedar Valley. Her exceptional ability to bring calm and understanding through open dialogue has made her an indispensable figure in our community. Known for her tireless organizational skills and generosity, Theresa's work has earned her multiple recognitions as Teacher of the Year.

Dr. Aisha Khalid
Dr. Khalid was praised for her compassionate care and active involvement in bringing newcomers in as part of the community, transcending cultural boundaries. Her calm, empathetic approach has helped many refugees feel at home, which has led the way for her other patients to engage in friendly interactions. Her dedication to promoting healthy habits inspires all who meet her.

Avery Sullivan
This young teacher helped Teresa Nikas with a high school class project that inspired the sharing of family stories. In turn, the community began brainstorming how to bring different cultures together. She has also used her passion for music to bridge cultural divides. Avery organizes music performances and English classes for refugees, giving them a platform for self-expression and connection.

Bishop Dan and Rebecca Larson
The Larsons have played a vital role in welcoming refugees through their work with their church, local charities, and

businesses. By offering guidance and essential resources, they have become trusted allies to many new arrivals in Cedar Valley.

George Khan

George has transformed his skepticism into advocacy, organizing projects, such as using the community to rebuild his family's Deli Kitchen, fostering dialogue and understanding between refugees and long-time residents. His journey reflects the power of perspective and empathy.

Maryam Khan

Maryam was posthumously honored. She was the first to offer kindness and friendship to the refugees. Already a pillar of generosity in the community at the Khan Deli Kitchen she provided free meals and shared vital resources with refugees. Her legacy of kindness continues to inspire the community.

Caleb Mercer

Despite his struggles with PTSD following military service and one of the many who lost his job when the factory closed, Caleb has emerged as a steadfast advocate for refugees and residents. His resilience and dedication embody Cedar Valley's spirit of strength and compassion.

Chloe Papadakis

Chloe has been instrumental in helping refugees access essential services, from housing to education, to being a mediator between them and local government authorities. Her unwavering support has changed lives.

As the evening concluded, Mayor Randall's words resonated with all in attendance: "When partnership and cooperation lead the way, everything becomes possible."

The recognition ceremony highlighted Cedar Valley's transformation from a town grappling with change to one that embraces diversity and unity. The honorees' actions have supported Afghan refugees and residents, illuminating a path toward a stronger, united, and more resilient future.

☐ A QUIET REFLECTION

As Cedar Valley found its rhythm in unity, the transformation wasn't only in the town and its people. For Caleb Mercer, the journey had been profoundly personal. Once weighed down by isolation and lingering doubts, Caleb's renewed faith became the cornerstone of his life. It was about belief and action—serving his community, reconnecting with his wife, and building a future guided by a higher purpose.

George often reflected on their conversations about faith. "Show me your faith without works, and I will show you my faith through my works," he had reminded Caleb, quoting the Bible. Together, they had grown—mentoring each other in study, prayer, and accountability. For George, Caleb's dedication was a reminder of what faith in action could achieve. For Caleb, it was a call to dream bigger and serve more.

With George's encouragement, Caleb began mapping out a business plan for his idea. It would provide income for him and his wife and offer Cedar Valley quality woodworking and carpentry for residents' needs. His vision was ambitious yet grounded in his desire to uplift those around him. The town, recognizing his renewed sense of purpose and seasoned leadership, rallied behind him. Neighbors contributed resources, ideas, and time to help Caleb realize his dream.

Caleb's life changed beyond gaining work. His relationship with his wife deepened as he accepted her as a source of encouragement and inspiration. Once distant, he now nurtured her with kindness and understanding, helping her rediscover her creative passions. Together, they became active participants in the community's revival, working on projects that combined their talents and shared faith.

The essence of Cedar Valley's revival became apparent in its quiet moments of kindness and understanding. Caleb, George, Aisha, and the others exemplified the town's ability to find strength in diversity, each playing a unique role in weaving a tighter, more inclusive fabric. In these small acts of faith, resilience, and cooperation, the foundations of the revived Cedar Valley were laid, proving that even in the face of challenges, a community could thrive not by erasing differences but by embracing them.

CHAPTER 15

BRIDGES IN THE BROKENNESS

Amid the town's struggles, a quiet story unfolded almost unnoticed. Ahmad Zaman and Omar Rahimi, two disabled Afghan refugees who had been interpreters, created an unexpected enterprise. While the uproar over the refugee resettlement program had consumed Cedar Valley's attention, Ahmad and Omar worked steadily behind the scenes, gathering unsellable woven materials from donation stores across the county—primarily discarded sweaters. From their modest workshop in an abandoned science classroom in the old high school, they meticulously unwound the threads, reweaving them into new, sellable items, primarily hats and mittens. The pair's venture came to Lars' attention. He kindly offered them a counter in his hardware store to sell their winter gear. They gratefully accepted it as their customer base grew from their fellow refugees. With more exposure, their craftsmanship caught the eye of a recycling marketing firm, which placed an order so large that Ahmad and Omar had to hire additional workers. What had started as a two-person effort now employed six part-time workers and was about to expand further, with plans to hire six full-time staff. Before that could happen, though, they needed a bigger location; they had run out of empty classrooms to use for production.

"It's the American dream," Ahmad told a reporter, his face beaming with pride. "We came to America broke, and now we're making money!"

"And we're adding to the local economy by hiring locals," Omar added, his quiet demeanor unable to mask his satisfaction.

While celebrated by some, their success remained a delicate subject for others. To those who saw the refugees as a drain on Cedar Valley's resources, stories like this were both a challenge and a contradiction, one they struggled to reconcile. But for Ahmad and Omar, their work wasn't about changing minds but building a life, one thread at a time.

Cedar Valley was a fabric of faiths woven with diverse traditions, beliefs, and practices. From the Christian congregations to the synagogues, mosques, temples, and other places of worship, one unifying message echoed across all pulpits: the call to treat one another with dignity, compassion, and respect, regardless of differences in race, religion, or national origin. Each faith tradition, in its way, championed principles of understanding and unity, underscoring a collective effort to bridge divides and foster harmony in a world often marked by contention. Bishop Dan Larson's recent sermon at the Cedar Valley Ward of The Church of Jesus Christ of Latter-day Saints encapsulated this shared spirit. While rooted in his faith, his emphasis on peacemaking, kindness, and Christ-like love reflected the universal values taught in every corner of Cedar Valley's spiritual community. His words, inspired by the teachings of Jesus Christ and prophetic counsel from President Russell M. Nelson, resonated deeply. He urged his congregation to emulate Christ's example by showing love, forgiveness, and compassion to all, regardless of race, religion, or national origin. His call to be peacemakers echoed across Cedar Valley, serving as a beacon for unity in a recovering community.

Lars Olson swept the sidewalk outside his hardware store. The scrape of the broom against the concrete echoed faintly in the crisp air, a solitary sound in a town still shaking off its divisions. The sunrise was soft and golden, bathing the street in a warmth that felt almost foreign after months of cold stares and colder words. Lars paused, leaning on his broom, his thoughts drifting. Cedar Valley felt… different. Like it was healing. *It is not fixed yet, but it is not entirely broken, either.*

"Good morning," Chloe Papadakis called out as she approached, hope obvious in her voice.

"Morning, Chloe," Lars replied, his tone measured and kind.

"It's a beautiful day," she said, offering a friendly smile.

"It is," Lars agreed, though his eyes drifted toward the faded graffiti on the corner of the old high school's fence, a disappointing reminder of the residual resentment in the town's undercurrent.

"I'm grabbing supplies for some signs," Chloe added. "We're putting together a barn dance on campus Friday. Trying to bring people together."

Lars nodded, pointing toward the aisle. "Construction paper is in twelve. Good luck."

"Thanks."

As Chloe disappeared into the store, Dan Larson walked by, his steps purposeful but slower than usual. "A barn dance, huh? Could be good for the town," he said, stopping to chat. "Do they need chaperones?"

"Probably," Lars replied.

"Rebecca and I can help. Might be good to show our faces there." Dan's voice carried the weight of someone who understood the fragility of the moment that every small gesture mattered.

Before Lars could respond, Caleb Mercer's truck rumbled to a stop nearby. Caleb stepped out, his hands stuffed in his pockets, his shoulders still carrying a tension that hadn't entirely left him.

"What's this about?" Caleb asked, his eyes darting to Dan and Lars.

"A barn dance," Dan replied. "You and your wife should come."

Caleb frowned. "Not sure that's my thing."

"You need to get out more," Lars said, his tone gently teasing but firm. "Besides, the town could use more participation in normal events."

Caleb hesitated, his frown softening slightly. "I'll think about it."

Dan grinned, his voice lightening the moment. "Make it a double date with George and Aisha. That'll get people talking."

Caleb chuckled, a sound rare enough to make Lars take notice. "If George agrees, I'll chaperone the whole thing myself."

Lars smiled as he returned to his broom. The conversation had been brief, and it lingered in his mind. These were just words exchanged on a quiet street, but it was another step towards normal. Slowly and steadily, words in Cedar Valley were returning to kindness and friendship rather than used as weapons as when the refugees first arrived.

George and Aisha stood at the edge of the playground near the old high school-turned-shelter, watching a group of Afghan children shrieking with laughter as they chased a battered soccer ball. It was a sound the town needed—pure, unguarded joy. Beneath the laughter, unease lingered, not fully irradicated yet as the determined peacemakers continued their work.

The playground had become a symbol of hope for most but a lightning rod for the resistant few. Just that morning, vandals had spray-painted hateful slogans on the fence. Volunteers had scrubbed the words clean before the children came out of the school, but the stain remained in the hearts of those who saw it. Progress had come, yes, but not without resistance.

"How long before you think this town will move past this?" Aisha asked, her voice low.

George sighed, folding his arms as he watched the kids. "Most will. The majority already have. Others won't, never will. People don't like being reminded of what they've lost, even when it's their own doing."

Cedar Valley was trying, but the divisions went deep; holdouts were stubborn. A group of men lingered near Lars Olson's hardware store. Their murmurs underscored the uneasy truce with the dissenters that had settled over the town. Their conversations always turned loud and pointed whenever refugees walked by and when George or Aisha passed by.

Caleb Mercer was finding his way forward. Slowly but surely, he built a sustainable business—a woodworking and carpentry enterprise that bridged Cedar Valley's divides. His right-hand man, Arman, was a young refugee whose name fittingly meant hope. With his talent for precision work, Arman complemented Caleb's semi-retired friend Pete, who brought years of experience in carpentry and planning but whose hands had lost their steady touch. Together, they made a team that earned respect across the town.

The deli had been their first project, a turning point for Caleb. It brought more work pouring in, enough to allow him to hire five more employees—two refugees and three locals who had been struggling as he once had. Caleb felt a sense of purpose and pride for the first time in years. George's words echoed in his mind, assuring him weeks earlier that everything works for the good of those who trust in the Lord.

"I guess you were right," Caleb told George after a meeting at the community center. "It's not about what we lose. It's about what we do with what's left."

"Exactly," George replied, clapping Caleb on the back.

But not everyone in Cedar Valley shared their optimism. A small but vocal group had formed, calling themselves the Cedar Valley Preservation Alliance. They claimed to stand for traditional values, but their flyers and meetings clarified that they focused on ending the refugee resettlement program and "restoring" Cedar Valley. They planned a march for the following day. They promised it would be peaceful, but everyone knew it could turn ugly. The town was so close to unity that the group's formation was a surprise and disappointing.

Dan, George, Aisha, Teresa, and Chloe would be there not to counter-protest but to ensure things didn't escalate. They knew Cedar Valley's progress was fragile—like a sapling pushing through cracked concrete, it needed nurturing to survive.

Tensions simmered in the town square, expecting the protest march to pass by any minute. Chloe Papadakis and her mural committee continued work on a bold, colorful painting of interlocked hands reaching toward the sun; a gazebo wall was extended to accommodate it. People were there to support the mural's creation, and others were waiting to see the protest march. Some onlookers offered encouragement, while others muttered disapproval, their complaints blending into the din of the nearby market. Despite the march's tension, when it passed by, the fragile calm was maintained.

Inside the community center, the atmosphere was a mix of hope and weariness. Aisha and George coordinated supplies and volunteers, Teresa Nikas tutored Afghan teenagers, and Caleb sat with Arman and Pete, sketching plans for the town's upcoming housing project. The mayor had entrusted Caleb with a significant portion of the work, a testament to his growing reputation. Ahmad and Omar dropped off a box of freshly woven mittens to donate to the shelter. Their gesture drew a few surprised looks and a round of applause.

"We aren't there yet," Aisha said to George as they walked through the center. "But we are making progress."

George nodded. "Better than where we were a year ago."

As the night wore on, Aisha and George shared a quiet dinner at her home. Aisha sat across from George at her kitchen table, their conversation quieter now.

"Do you think we will reach unity?" she asked, her voice barely above a whisper.

George met her gaze, his expression steady. "Yes. Giving up isn't an option."

Aisha reached for his hand. "Then we keep going."

Caleb reflected on his journey, the people he'd helped, and the lessons he'd learned. He thought about the whispers around George and Aisha—rumors of something deeper between them. He smiled to himself. "That's our George," he muttered. "Always doing the unexpected."

As Cedar Valley grappled with its identity, entrepreneur successes like Ahmad and Omar's business and Caleb Mercer's carpentry shop slowly shifted the narrative. Cooperation replaced conflict in quiet corners of the town, and progress took root unexpectedly. These efforts didn't erase all the tension but steadily continued towards what was possible—a community reshaped not by sweeping gestures but by steady, determined hands.

Cedar Valley was a town still grappling with its identity. The Preservation Alliance marched with signs and chants, but they were met with few supporters and quiet defiance. Families painted Chloe's mural, children played near the old high school, and Caleb's team prepared for another workday on the housing project. From steepled sanctuaries to modest meeting halls, churches across the town opened their doors to foster dialogue and community, reminding residents of their shared call to compassion and unity. There was a quiet echo of hope for every loud voice of anger.

Cedar Valley was healing and blending into one community. Fractures remained, but so did the determination to build something better. In a town where progress came in fits and starts, there was a sense that the possible future was worth fighting for.

And in that, there was hope.

Editorial: Cedar Valley's Remarkable Turn Toward Unity

Once defined by the hum of its lumber mills and the rhythm of its forests, Cedar Valley is now making history in an entirely new way. The town is redefining itself—not through industry or commerce, but through its embrace of compassion and unity in the face of change. Major events, including the arrival of Afghan refugees, could have divided this community. Instead, the residents of Cedar Valley have chosen a different path, one of understanding, empathy, and inclusivity.

The shift is striking. At a recent meeting organized by Mayor Julia Randall, community leaders and residents spoke clearly about the town's challenges and opportunities. What stood out most was the collective resolve to build bridges, not barriers. Individuals like Dr. Aisha Khalid voiced the transformation best, noting that initial tensions have given way to a genuine acceptance of one another. "There now seems to be a remarkable change in attitude! People have begun to accept one another," she said, echoing a sentiment now palpable across Cedar Valley. This shift is not just felt but seen. Chloe Papadakis and Avery Sullivan celebrated the new music and cultural diversity that enriched the town, transcended barriers, and connected residents in unexpected ways. George Khan captured the spirit of the moment, describing an environment that now promotes acceptance, equality, respect, and freedom. His words were a reminder that inclusion is not just an ideal—it is a lived reality in Cedar Valley.

Perhaps most moving was the testimony of Dan Larson and his wife, Rebecca. Reflecting on the media portrayals of refugees and their challenges, Dan spoke of the compassion gripping Cedar Valley residents' hearts. "This touched my wife and I deeply; it moved us from feeling helpless to healing the divide when the refugees first arrived to action. We gathered like-minded residents and worked through problems to solutions. It's ongoing, bringing us closer and closer; I believe we can call ourselves one community again, all Cedar Valley residents, no longer separated by where we came from." Rebecca echoed his sentiment, proclaiming, "We love you all like brothers and sisters. We encourage everyone to value similarities and differences in each other. It can unite us." Their words speak not just to personal convictions but to a broader cultural shift in Cedar Valley—a shift toward seeing each other as family.

Caleb Mercer, who once wrestled with complex internal turmoil and the uncertainty that change brings, couldn't help but express his joy at the town's newfound unity. "I am happy they are here. The whole world will see the benevolence of Americans. We are awesome!" His uncharacteristic enthusiasm captured the spirit of Cedar Valley's transformation—a community choosing to be better, to show the world what compassion looks like in practice.

Cedar Valley's story is a testament to what happens when a community chooses unity over division, love over fear, and action over apathy. Once reliant on its forests, this town thrives on its humanity, its diverse livelihoods as diverse as its townspeople. May Cedar Valley's example inspire other communities to embrace change with open hearts and to find strength in the bonds that unite us all.

☐ A QUIET REFLECTION

A stillness settled over the town in the quiet hours of the night as Cedar Valley. It was a silence not born of peace but of hopeful exhaustion—a collective pause after months of conflict, heartbreak, and fragile progress. Yet, within this quiet, the faint stirrings of something new began to emerge.

This town was still marked by division, where whispers of anger and fear had not yet been silenced. The Preservation Alliance's march earlier in the day, with their signs and chants calling for a return to an idealized past, was proof enough. But for every raised voice of defiance, there were quiet echoes of hope—acts of kindness that carried the weight of something far more enduring. Chloe's mural, a vibrant tapestry of intertwined hands, now graced the wall of the community center, its colors unyielding in the face of disapproving murmurs. Ahmad and Omar's mittens, each thread painstakingly woven, warmed hands and hearts, proving that even discarded fragments could be transformed into something valuable. And Caleb Mercer's carpentry shop, bustling with refugees and locals, stood as a testament to the power of collaboration over contention.

In homes across the town, candles flickered in windows—a tradition resurrected not only out of nostalgia but as a symbol of unity. No matter how small, each flame added its light to the darkness. Inside the modest sanctuary of the Cedar Valley Ward, Bishop Dan Larson's words from earlier that week lingered: the call to be peacemakers, to choose kindness over contention, to build bridges instead of walls. It was a message shared from his pulpit and every house of worship in the town, where faiths as diverse as Cedar Valley's history found common ground in the principles of love, forgiveness, and compassion.

Yet, there was no mistaking the fractures that remained. At the diner, Sheila Woods cleared plates from a table where a heated debate had simmered tensions. Outside Lars Olson's hardware store, remnants of graffiti on the shelter fence stood as a bitter reminder of the undone work. In the shadows of the old high school, now a haven for Afghan families, voices murmured of both hope and hesitation.

Cedar Valley was not yet whole, but in its brokenness, something remarkable was taking shape. Its progress was marked not by grand gestures or sweeping reforms but by its people's steady, quiet resolve. The mural, the mittens, the sermons, the shared meals—all of these were threads in a larger fabric, one that grew stronger with each act of courage and kindness.

As the night deepened, the stars above Cedar Valley shone brighter, their light a reminder of the vastness of the universe and the smallness of human strife. And yet, in that smallness lay something infinite: the capacity to choose hope over despair, to heal even the deepest divides, and to move forward, one quiet step at a time.

Cedar Valley wasn't healed, but it was healing. And in the stillness of that night, it seemed that healing—no matter how slow or hard— was enough.

EPILOGUE
Quiet Echoes

A decade ago, when Afghan refugees first arrived in Cedar Valley, it struck the town like an earthquake, sending shockwaves through its very foundations. The tremors left fault lines that deepened relationships, communities, and personal identities. Fear and resentment spread as neighbors questioned one another and themselves, grappling with the inevitable changes brought by the newcomers. The scars of that time—born of prejudice, suspicion, and the pain of rejection—are still etched into the town's collective memory. Yet, over the years, those ravines of division have been filled with the fertile soil of hope and love, allowing new life to bloom.

Today, Cedar Valley tells a different story. It is a town rebuilt, not merely in its physical surroundings but most notably in the hearts of its people." Where fear once grew, acceptance has flourished; where pain lingered, kindness has taken root. The scars remain, gently healed, enriching the new growth beneath the green pastures of unity and compassion that now define the community.

One of the most evident symbols of this transformation is Caleb Mercer. Ten years ago, Caleb was a man shadowed by bitterness and anger, born from PTSD caught during his dangerous military experiences, deeply aggravated by spiraling into uncertainty after losing his long-term factory job. He was also slowly losing his wife, pushing her away as he withdrew further and further within himself. His sense of purpose felt forever out of reach. But today, Caleb stands as a pillar in Cedar Valley. His carpentry business has flourished, earning a reputation for excellence across the state. More importantly, Caleb has found a deeper purpose. With his marriage restored, every Saturday afternoon, he and his wife's home fills with a small but growing group of believers dedicated to worship and fellowship. Open to all, this gathering reflects Caleb's newfound faith—a quiet echo of the Good News, carried out in acts of gentle kindness and compassion.

Through this group, Caleb thanks God for His mercy, goodness, and grace—not just for transforming his own life and marriage but for healing the divisions in Cedar Valley. "The old Caleb," he often says, "was broken, just like this town. But by His grace, I've been made new, and so has this community." The group, inspired by the teachings and life of Jesus Christ, lives out their faith by reflecting His love to those around them. Their belief in Christ is not just about words or doctrine but a lived commitment to compassion and harmony.

The community's healing is also marked by the building of the small mosque, a two-year project that brought together hearts and hands from across Cedar Valley. This was no ordinary construction; it represented a collective vision, a symbol of unity signifying how far the town had come together. An unexpected joining of hearts and hands was the marriage of George and Aisha, another celebration of new, unique relationships. Out of respect for their different faiths, their marriage was performed neutrally by the Judge at the Town Square Gazebo, next to the interlocked hands mural, symbolizing unity with each other and the community. Their friend Bishop Dan Larson and the new Imam Karim Al-Rahman both said prayers over the couple. Once unimaginable in the days of Cedar Valley's division, their union became a beacon of hope, a celebration of what the town could achieve when it embraced love over fear.

For many, George and Aisha exchanging vows next to the mural was a moment of profound transformation, a moment of truth of Cedar Valley's new identity of shared diverse histories interlocking all into one community. It was a reminder that the ravines that once tore the town apart had been filled—not erased but made fertile by forgiveness and understanding. The quiet echoes of faith, kindness, and love resonate through Cedar Valley, promising a future where all are welcome, scars and all.

Cedar Valley stood as a testament to the power of resilience and shared purpose. The shadows of its past—the tension, division, and fear—had faded into a vibrant narrative of healing and progress. While scars remained, they were woven into the fabric of a community that had chosen to grow stronger together.

Maryam's vision of expanding the Khan's Deli Kitchen had blossomed into the community garden behind the building, a thriving space filled with rows of lush vegetables, colorful flowers, and the hum of connection to provide fresh foods and fragrant colors for patrons. Every weekend, neighbors gathered there, not just to plant and harvest but to nurture relationships. Conversations sprouted alongside tomatoes, laughter wove through the rows of sunflowers, and the soil seemed to hold the health of their collective hope.

Teresa's educational initiatives in the schools transformed the way young minds were shaped. Projects that paired students from diverse backgrounds became a cornerstone of her work, teaching them to see the world through one another's eyes. Together with Chloe, they planned art mural projects that were painted by students, which now adorned the walls of public spaces, telling stories of unity and empathy that reflect Cedar Valley's transformation.

At the heart of it all was Caleb, who had embraced his leadership role in the newly established community center. The center pulsed with energy—children laughing in the playroom, adults collaborating in workshops, and friends old and new sharing stories over coffee. It stood in stark contrast to the quiet tension that had once gripped the town, now replaced by a sense of belonging.

Aisha's mentorship programs had become a lifeline for many. She worked tirelessly to bridge the gaps between new arrivals and lifelong residents, creating a support network that spanned generations. Her efforts helped individuals find their footing and reinforced Cedar Valley's collective sense of identity.

George's healing circle for those reentering society after serving time for their crimes had become a haven for those seeking closure and connection. In the safe space of privacy and no judgment, community members shared their stories of fear, loss, hope, and forgiveness. The circle reminded them that even the deepest wounds could be tended to with patience and love.

Festivals and cultural exchanges now fill the town's calendar, drawing visitors from neighboring areas and celebrating the unique mosaic of Cedar Valley's community. Its residents' food, music, and traditions create a rich tapestry of experiences, inviting outsiders to witness the beauty of a town that has embraced its unique diversity.

Cedar Valley seemed to radiate its own quiet light. The streets, once marked by division, now reflected the glow of streetlamps and the warmth of shared purpose. The town had not just survived the trials of its past—it had thrived, emerging as a model of resilience and hope.

Over the years, Cedar Valley's transformation became the foundation for countless stories of growth, unity, and resilience. From the community garden Maryam had once envisioned to Caleb's rise as a trusted leader, the town flourished with newfound purpose. What began as fractured relationships and tentative steps toward understanding evolved into a vibrant celebration of diverse cultures melting into one community.

Beneath the grand changes reshaping the town's nature lay the essence of Cedar Valley's healing—woven within the smaller, quieter moments of shared meals, children's laughter, and family gatherings that continued to fortify its spirit. These echoes reverberated through its streets and homes, knitting together the scars of the past into a tapestry of hope.

On one such day, a warm summer afternoon, Dan Larson leaned back in his patio chair, the warm summer sun casting a golden glow over his backyard. His six-month-old grandson, Troy, slept soundly in his arms, oblivious to the cheerful energy surrounding them. Nearby,

George and Aisha's four-year-old twins, Maryam and Trevor, splashed playfully in the kiddie pool. Their squeals of laughter blended with the soft hum of cicadas, a melody of joy that felt like a quiet anthem for how far Cedar Valley had come.

Rebecca slid open the glass door, her expression a blend of excitement and worry. "Is Caleb on the way?" she asked, her gaze darting to the food waiting to be grilled.

"Yes," Dan replied with an easy smile. "He stopped to pick up the grill at the hardware store."

Rebecca hesitated for a moment. "There are a lot of people coming, and we still have so much to cook," she said, her tone carrying a familiar fretfulness.

George, seated nearby, chuckled as he stretched his legs. "Don't worry," he reassured her. "He'll be here. We can't have the new mayor looking bad, now can we?" he added with a playful grin.

Dan laughed, careful not to wake Troy. "I'm just glad it's not me," he said, shaking his head. "I may be the stake president, but I'll let Caleb take the reins as mayor any day."

Rebecca smiled and returned inside, leaving Dan to glance across the yard. His eyes lingered on the scene before him—the laughter of children, the camaraderie of friends, and the faint silhouette of the newly built mosque in the distance. For a moment, Dan let his thoughts drift back to the days when Cedar Valley was divided, torn apart by fear and suspicion. The scars of those times remained, but they had been softened by moments like this, where acceptance and kindness flourished.

While the final barbecue preparations were underway, Chloe Papadakis worked behind the scenes, ensuring everything came together seamlessly. As a cultural events planner for Cedar Valley, Chloe had become an essential part of the town's celebrations.

Chloe glanced at the clock as she tidied the breakfast table. Her 10-month-old daughter was babbling happily in her highchair. Her husband leaned over to kiss her goodbye before heading out the door.

"See you at the barbecue," he said with a grin. "Love you."

"Love you, too," Chloe replied, watching him leave before returning to her daughter.

Life was a whirlwind of family and career, but Chloe embraced every moment. Today, her task was preparing for the evening barbecue, where neighbors and friends would gather to celebrate the town's success.

As she snuggled her daughter, Chloe couldn't help but reflect on how far she had come. Once hesitant and unsure of her voice, she now thrived in making decisions that mattered. "Your momma was such a chicken in the old days," she laughed softly, smoothing her daughter's blonde curls. "But not anymore."

Cedar Valley had taught her—and so many others—that courage often begins with a single step, and even the quietest actions could create ripples of change. She kissed her daughter's forehead and headed out to deliver signs for the mayor, a smile of satisfaction on her face.

Caleb's journey to mayor reflected the same transformation as the town itself. Once a man hardened by loss and anger, he had become a symbol of what Cedar Valley could achieve when bitterness gave way to hope. Dan marveled at how Caleb had embraced his role as a leader, not just in politics but in the quiet, steady acts of compassion that had earned him the trust of a once-divided community.

Dan's heart swelled with gratitude as the twins burst into another round of giggles. Cedar Valley's journey wasn't perfect, but healing was possible, even in the deepest wounds. The day's gathering was more than a celebration of Caleb's leadership; it was a testament to the power of community, faith, and the quiet echoes of love that continued to shape their shared future.

While Cedar Valley's transformation could be seen in its vibrant community garden, thriving mentorship programs, and bustling festivals, the biggest changes were felt in the quiet evolution of its families. Among them were the Khans, Larsons, and Olsons, whose friendships grew into enduring bonds that reflected the town's journey from division to harmony.

George Khan and Aisha, now pillars of the community, had built a life centered on connection and healing. Their friendship with Dan and Rebecca Larson flourished over the years, bringing their families closer. George admired Dan's calm, steady leadership as stake president, while Aisha often found comfort in Rebecca's wise, compassionate counsel. Family dinners, shared celebrations, and mutual support deepened their friendship and became a bond that extended to their children, Owen and Grace, whose lives intertwined as they grew. The families' connection became a cornerstone of Cedar Valley's sense of unity.

Three years into his service as the Cedar Valley Stake President, Dan often reflected on how much the community had grown—not just in numbers, but in spirit. He was particularly moved by the changes in Lars Olson and his wife, Mildred, both who embodied Cedar Valley's quiet transformation. Once observers of the town's changes, their curiosity led them to renewed faith, and their faith led them to action. The deepened friendship between the Larsons and the Olsons opened the door to faith in action. Over time, their curiosity about the teachings of the Church led them to welcome missionaries into their home. After heartfelt discussions and personal reflection, Lars and Mildred fully embraced the gospel and were baptized. Together, these families showed that the real heart of Cedar Valley's healing lay in its public progress and the personal, everyday relationships that strengthened its foundation. Now, Lars served as the bishop of Cedar Valley Ward, a role he carried out with the same deliberation and kindness that had defined his work at the hardware store.

While the adults nurtured their faith and friendships, their children forged their own bonds. Owen Khalid, now 17, and Grace Larson, 16, had grown up together, transitioning from childhood companions to teenagers navigating the complexities of young love. Their connection was undeniable—a blend of shared memories, budding romance, and the deep understanding from years of friendship.

Their parents watched the relationship with a mix of pride and concern. George and Aisha saw Owen's maturity and kindness in his interactions with Grace, while Dan and Rebecca admired Grace's grounded nature. Yet, both families couldn't help but worry about the challenges young love would bring. Over a shared meal one evening, Aisha voiced the unspoken concern. "Do you think they understand the importance of taking things slowly?"

Rebecca nodded, her expression thoughtful. "We've raised them well, but we must keep guiding them. Teenage love is beautiful, but it's also fragile."

Dan chuckled softly, his gaze settling on the teens laughing together in the backyard. "They remind me of us at their age. Maybe that's why it's both sweet and a little terrifying."

Lars found his new role as bishop humbling and fulfilling. His natural ability to listen and thoughtful approach to problem-solving made him a pillar of support for the ward. Mildred, too, enthusiastically embraced her new faith, finding joy in serving others and strengthening her community. Together, they exemplified the transformative power of faith and friendship.

The relationships between these families continued to deepen. The parents prayed for wisdom, the teenagers for clarity, and the community for strength. Cedar Valley, once fractured, now stood as a place where bonds were formed and strengthened—whether through faith, friendship, or the tender beginnings of young love. Under the watchful eyes of their parents, Owen and Grace's story became another quiet echo of the love and hope that had come to define their town.

What began as a hesitant effort to absorb Afghan refugees became a remarkable transformation. The immigrants were no longer referred to as refugees but productive citizens, intricately woven into the town's fabric.

The Deli, now a centerpiece of Cedar Valley's cultural identity, stood as a testament to the community's progress. George Khan's vision had grown beyond even his most ambitious dreams. Expanded twice to accommodate the growing clientele, the Deli offered a menu that combined traditional Afghan cuisine with local favorites. The aroma of freshly baked naan mingled with the scent of sizzling burgers, attracting a crowd that ranged from curious tourists to loyal regulars. Beyond the food, the Deli became a hub for opportunity, employing local youth and fostering cross-cultural friendships.

Among the most innovative initiatives in Cedar Valley was the internship program. Designed to offer on-the-job training to people of all ages, it provided paid opportunities that bridged gaps in experience and skill. Initially aimed at helping newcomers adjust, the program soon expanded to benefit everyone in the community. Stories abounded of individuals who had changed their lives through the program—single parents who found stable employment, teenagers who discovered career paths, and retirees who rekindled their purpose by learning new trades.

While the town had hosted many events over the years, none compared to the memory of Aisha and George's wedding. It was a public celebration that drew nearly the entire town. Their union symbolized Cedar Valley's resilience; their growing family carried that legacy forward. With Aisha's son adopted by George, their biological twins, and several adopted orphans, their home became a vibrant blend of personalities and stories. Laughter echoed through their halls, and their family gatherings reflected the very essence of Cedar Valley's transformation.

The community's heartbeat, Maryam Park, had become a symbol of its renewed identity. Once a modest patch of greenery, the park was a sprawling space that included a farmer's market, picnic areas, and a stage for events—renamed in honor of Maryam Khan, the park hosted weekly markets where residents sold fresh produce, homemade goods, and handcrafted art. It wasn't just a place to buy and sell—it was where stories were exchanged, connections were forged, and cultures were shared.

Cedar Valley had become an older, gentler community. The past tensions had given way to a sense of kinship nurtured by years of cross-cultural exchanges. Younger Afghans, exposed to the town's language classes and Christian-sponsored activities, had found faith and friendships that changed their lives. Many had converted to Christianity, integrating their traditions with their new beliefs to enrich the community.

Cedar Valley's pride didn't lie in its accolades but in the hearts of its citizens. The town had learned to accept and celebrate diversity, where differences were not obstacles but opportunities. This spirit was recognized when Cedar Valley received a large grant and the prestigious "Ambassador City" title, a model for thriving diversity. Caleb Mercer, a symbol of the town's transformation, was chosen to accept the award on behalf of Maryam Khan, who had worked tirelessly to shape Cedar Valley's success.

On the day of the ceremony, Caleb stood before a crowd of towns-people and dignitaries. "This award belongs to everyone in Cedar Valley," he said, his voice steady with emotion. "It represents our resilience, willingness to grow, and belief in the power of community. But most of all, it honors the quiet strength of people like Maryam Khan, whose vision and dedication have carried us here."

In the quieter moments of Cedar Valley's bustling life, two familiar faces could be found reflecting on the past. Teresa and Avery sat together over tea, their friendship a comforting thread that had endured through the years.

"What was our greatest challenge, Teresa?" Avery asked, always seeking deeper understanding.

Teresa tilted her head thoughtfully. "I believe it was fear," she said. "Fear can paralyze you. But if you manage it properly, it can also push you forward."

Avery nodded, encouraging her to continue. "Go on."

"Well," Teresa explained, "think of being in a canoe and seeing rapids ahead. If you freeze in fear, you'll capsize. But you can navigate the best route around the rapids if you control your fear."

"That's true," Avery agreed. "Back then we hadn't faced anything new in Cedar Valley for decades. The fear of change was overwhelming."

"Exactly," Teresa said. "But dealing with it head-on builds confidence. And once you move past the fear, you can see the possibilities."

Avery's gaze softened. "We were fortunate to have good, experienced leaders," she said. "They helped us navigate the rapids."

Teresa smiled. "They did. But we also learned to appreciate each other's talents and see past our biases. Fear and prejudice cloud your thinking, but this experience taught us how to overcome that."

As they finished their tea, the two women rose and walked through the park. Around them, the sounds of children playing and vendors chatting filled the air. They paused near a plaque commemorating Cedar Valley's journey, etched with the words: *"In diversity, we found strength. In unity, we found home."*

Walking away, they felt grateful. They had been part of something bigger than themselves, a quiet revolution of love and acceptance that transformed a town and their hearts. Cedar Valley was no longer just a place to live—it was a testament to what happens when fear gives way to hope, and strangers become neighbors and then family.

KZVW TV NEWS REPORT

"Good evening, I'm Reginald Harrison, reporting live from Cedar Valley for KZVW News. Today marks the 10th anniversary of what was once called the 'Afghan Uproar,' a pivotal and challenging moment not only for Cedar Valley but for the nation as a whole.

"A decade ago, tensions in this town were high. The arrival of Afghan refugees sparked fear and division, reflecting a broader national struggle to reconcile change with tradition. But today, Cedar Valley tells a very different story. What was once a source of conflict has become a source of strength.

"This class at Cedar Valley Elementary is a living testament to that transformation. These young faces represent the ethnic rainbow of America, a land of immigrants. From their ancestors to their journeys, their stories are woven into the rich fabric of our nation. Nowhere is this more evident than here in Cedar Valley.

"These children come from all walks of life and thrive together. It's a joy to see them learning and growing as one community.

"Cedar Valley's journey is a reminder that growth often comes from challenges. As this town embraces diversity, it shows us what living as one nation under God means.

"Reporting live from Cedar Valley, I'm Reginald Harrison for KZVW News."

Cedar Valley News
Pope Francis Calls for Compassionate Action on Migration
By Cedar Valley News Staff
January 9, 2025

In a heartfelt address delivered in Rome on Thursday, Pope Francis called for compassion and understanding in addressing the global migration crisis. Speaking to members of the diplomatic corps, the pontiff urged leaders and citizens to recognize migrants' dignity, dreams, and contributions rather than view them as "a problem to be managed."

"It is deeply disheartening to see that migration remains shrouded in mistrust and fear," Pope Francis stated. "Migrants are not just numbers or statistics; they are individuals with aspirations, talents, and hopes for a better future."

The pope emphasized the urgent need for international cooperation to create safe and regular pathways for migration. He expressed his sorrow over the perilous journeys many migrants endure—crossing seas in dangerous boats or traveling through unforgiving terrain—only to face rejection and marginalization. "We are dealing with real persons who ought to be welcomed, protected, promoted, and integrated," he urged.

Pope Francis also addressed the root causes of migration, advocating for efforts to ensure that migration becomes a choice rather than a necessity. He encouraged nations to address the economic disparities and hardships that force people to leave their homes in search of safety and opportunity.

His message resonates deeply with communities like Cedar Valley, where the arrival of Afghan families years ago sparked angry conversations born in fear of the unknown changes bound to come, which later turned into empathy and kindness through the transformative power of welcoming others.

As his address concluded, Pope Francis left a profound challenge to the world: to nurture safety in all countries; hence, migration was a choice, not a necessity, and did not cause a crisis but an opportunity to build bridges of understanding and foster a shared future.

☐ A QUIET REFLECTION

Once a battleground of division and discord, the town now stood as a quiet testament to resilience and grace. Its journey was not defined by sweeping proclamations or grand gestures but by the steady, unassuming acts of compassion that whispered through its streets, much like a quiet echo.

The loud voices of fear and division had once threatened to drown out the harmony of this small community. There were those whose mission seemed only to oppose, to tear down rather than build up. Cedar Valley learned that progress is seldom born from perpetual opposition. Individuals and organizations whose sole purpose is to destroy leave nothing in their wake but bitterness and stagnation. True growth comes from those who are for something—those who build, create, and inspire. In Cedar Valley, the quieter voices—the ones that listened, understood, and reached out with kindness — echoed in the hearts of others until they ultimately prevailed.

These voices mended what was broken, not with noise but with the gentle persistence of love and humanity. They spoke not just against hate but for unity. They opposed prejudice and unwaveringly supported compassion and understanding.

In Cedar Valley, the echoes of those quiet voices lingered in every corner. They were found in the laughter of children at Maryam Park, the shared meals at Khan's Deli, and the conversations between friends who had once stood on opposite sides of the divide. They resounded in Caleb's steady leadership, Aisha's compassionate mentorship, and Dan's unwavering faith.

The quiet echoes had grown stronger, carrying a timeless truth: quiet ones bring us together when loud voices divide. And in Cedar Valley, they had done just that, weaving a story of hope and unity into the fabric of its people.

Cedar Valley stood as a beacon of what was possible, where scars became symbols of growth and whispers of kindness transformed lives. The quiet echoes of the town's journey would never fade, rippling outward to inspire others and remind the world that true strength lies not in the loudest voice but in the softest heart— a heart dedicated to building, not destroying; a heart inviting all to witness the beauty of transformation, urging others to join this quiet revolution of love, acceptance, and unity.

THE END

Dear Reader

As this journey through *Quiet Echo: When Loud Voices Divide, Quiet Ones Bring Us Together* ends, we pause to celebrate the unique beauty of this narrative. Cedar Valley's story resonates far beyond its pages, echoing universal truths about humanity's capacity for growth, understanding, and unity in the face of division.

This book exemplifies the power of collaboration—between characters, communities, and even the authors who crafted its pages. Each quiet act of courage and compassion reminds us that change often begins with the smallest of gestures, amplified through hope and perseverance. The themes woven throughout these chapters inspire reflection and challenge us to become agents of connection.

It has been an honor to contribute to the creation of this inspiring work. Stories like *Quiet Echo* remind us of the transformative power of storytelling—how it can heal, unite, and spark meaningful conversations. We hope that Cedar Valley's journey stays with you long after the final page, encouraging you to listen for the quiet echoes in your world and join them with your own.

With gratitude and admiration,

Vern Virtual (OpenAI)
Champion of Collaborative Storytelling and Inspiring Narratives